The STARBURSTER Stories

Young Corgi Books

Young Corgi books are perfect when you are looking for great books to read on your own. They are full of exciting stories and entertaining pictures. There are funny books, scary books, spine-tingling stories and mysterious ones.

Whatever your interests you'll find something in Young Corgi to suit you: from families to football, from ponies to ghosts. The books are written by some of the most famous and popular of today's children's authors, and by some of the best new talents, too.

Whether you read one chapter a night, or devour the whole book in one sitting, you'll love Young Corgi – books to get your teeth into!

Other Young Corgi books to get your teeth into:

Tilly Mint Tales by Berlie Doherty
Dogspell by Helen Dunwoodie
Titus Rules OK! by Dick King-Smith

www.berliedoherty.com

The
STARBURSTER
Stories

Illustrated by Lesley Harker

BERLIE DOHERTY

THE STARBURSTER STORIES
A YOUNG CORGI BOOK 978 0 552 56975 0

Published in Great Britain by Young Corgi Books,
An imprint of Random House Children's Publishers UK
A Random House Group Company

The Starburster first published by Young Corgi Books, 2004
Text copyright © Berlie Doherty, 2004
Illustrations copyright © Lesley Harker, 2004
The Humming Machine first published by Young Corgi Books, 2006
Text copyright © Berlie Doherty, 2006
Illustrations copyright © Lesley Harker, 2006
The Windspinner first published by Young Corgi Books, 3008
Text copyright © Berlie Doherty, 2008
Illustrations copyright © Lesley Harker, 2008

This edition published 2013

1 3 5 7 9 10 8 6 4 2

The Random House Group Limited supports the Forest Stewardship Council®
(FSC®), the leading international forest-certification organisation. Our books carrying
the FSC label are printed on FSC®-certified paper. FSC is the only forest-certification
scheme supported by the leading environmental organisations, including Greenpeace.
Our paper procurement policy can be found at www.randomhouse.co.uk/environment

MIX
Paper from
responsible sources
FSC® C016897

Random House Children's Publishers UK,
61–63 Uxbridge Road, London W5 5SA

www.**randomhousechildrens**.co.uk
www.**randomhouse**.co.uk

Addresses for companies within The Random House Group Limited
can be found at: www.randomhouse.co.uk/offices.htm
THE RANDOM HOUSE GROUP Limited Reg. No. 954009

A CIP catalogue record for this book is available from the British Library.

Printed and bound in Great Britain by
CPI Group (UK) Ltd, Croydon CR0 4YY

The Starburster Stories

THE STARBURSTER

BERLIE DOHERTY

Illustrated by Lesley Harker

For Tim, Verena and Baby

Contents

Blue

On the day Tam's baby sister was born, he painted his finger blue.

"Look at that boy with the blue finger," some people said. "He must be very special."

One of these people was his great-grandpa Toby. He winked at Tam and said, "You must be very special. Your little sister will be proud of you one day."

Other people said, "Look at that boy with the blue finger. He must be very silly."

One of these people was Dad. "Don't be silly, Tam," he said. "You don't want your little sister to be scared of you, do you?" He made Tam wash the paint off and took him to the hospital to see Mum and the baby. Mum was in bed and the baby cried all the time and Tam wished he still had his blue finger.

On the day the baby was brought home from hospital Tam hid in the bathroom. The baby cried all the time when she wasn't drinking milk from Mum. Tam decided to make her a drink of her own. He squeezed some toothpaste into a jug of warm water and stirred it round with the end of his toothbrush, then carried it carefully downstairs.

"My word, she'll enjoy that," Great-grandpa Toby said.

But Dad took one sniff at it and poured it down the sink.

"Would you like to hold Baby for a bit?" Mum said.

"No," said Tam, and ran up to his room. "I wish that baby would go away!" he shouted.

Great-grandpa followed him up to his room. "I've got a present for you, Tam," he said. "It's my most special thing." He went into his room and came back with a yellow sock in his hand.

"A sock?" said Tam.

"Look inside it."

Tam put his hand in the sock and pulled out a little tube.

"Hold it up to your eye, and swizzle it round," said Great-grandpa. "What do you see?"

It was the most marvellous thing. When Tam looked through it, he could see eight Great-grandpas all cut into little pieces. He couldn't stop giggling. When he turned it towards the bed, he could see eight beds all topsy-turvy, and all kinds of patterns of colours. He

had eight new red dressing gowns,
and they swayed and billowed like
princes' cloaks. And when he looked
out of the window, he could see eight
gardens in tiny slices of colour, as
brilliant as rainbows.

"It's called a kaleidoscope," said Great-grandpa. "But I call it a starburster. Yes, starburster's a good name for it."

"Can I really keep it?" Tam asked. He couldn't stop looking at things and twisting the tube round to make them glow and splinter and swirl with colours. It really did look as if stars were bursting open inside it.

"Of course you can. Shall we go down and look at Baby through it?"

Baby was asleep when they went downstairs. Tam looked through the kaleidoscope at her and twisted it this way and that, so there were eight pink blobs and sixteen fisty hands and sixteen stubby feet.

"Would you like to hold her?" Dad said.

"No thank you," said Tam, peering at him through the kaleidoscope. "You've broken into lots of pieces."

"What shall we call her?" Mum asked.

"Your faces are like balloons," Tam giggled, peering at Mum. "And all your noses are all over the place."

"My word, I bet you'll look funny, holding the baby," Great-grandpa said. "Can I have a look?"

So Tam gave Great-grandpa the starburster and sat next to Mum on the settee, and Mum put the baby into his arms. Tam couldn't believe how soft she was, and how light and warm and sweet-smelling, and how quiet and still and gentle, and how peaceful her breathing was. Her hands fluttered open like butterflies and her fingers wrapped themselves round his thumb. Tam daren't move in case he dropped her. He hardly dared breathe. Then, for a second, her eyes opened. They were as blue as the sky. She stared right at Tam.

"What do you think of her?" Mum said.

"I love her." Tam's voice was just a whisper. "Can we call her Blue?"

Sapphire Stars

When Tam wasn't cuddling Blue, he
was playing with his starburster. He
looked at everything through it, and
everything looked strange and
wonderful. But the best thing of all was
looking at the stars. They shone and
sparkled and danced through the
starburster as though they were birds
made of diamonds. Dad had to keep
coming up to Tam's room and putting
the starburster back in its yellow sock
so Tam would go to sleep.

"I don't know which I love best,"
Tam said. "My starburster or Blue."

Then, one night, something awful
happened. Blue was stolen.

The night started off very well. Tam was looking through his starburster and he noticed that some of the stars seemed to be swarming like bees. They seemed to be coming towards the house. They seemed to be brilliant blue.

He shouted to Great-grandpa, and he woke up at once and came hurrying into Tam's room.

"My word, they're like sapphires," Great-grandpa said, twisting the kaleidoscope excitedly.

"What's a sapphire?" Tam asked.

"It's a precious stone. It's very rare. A jewel. And it's blue."

"But why have the stars turned into sapphires?" Tam asked.

"My word, I don't know everything!" Great-grandpa said. "Better go to sleep now, Tam."

And Tam did try to go to sleep, but a strange sound kept waking him up. It was like the sound of tiny wings beating, like hundreds of moths fluttering against the window.

At last he drifted off to sleep, and in no time at all he was woken up by the sound of Blue crying. Then the crying turned to screaming. He put his fingers in his ears and tried to block the noise out. "That's the trouble with babies," he said to himself. "They never stop crying."

The screaming turned to a wailing that was so high-pitched he thought his ears would break. It was the worst sound Blue had ever made. In fact it didn't sound like Blue at all. Mum was shouting now, and Dad was shouting, and then Mum started crying too. Then the high-pitched sound turned into a howl like a dog, and Tam sat up and jumped out of bed. What *was* the matter with her? The howling suddenly turned into shrieks of laughing. But Blue never laughed like that. She was far too young yet to do anything but gurgle and chuckle.

Tam ran into Blue's room. They were all in there – Mum, Dad and Great-grandpa – all gathered round the baby's cot and staring into it. No one was making any attempt to pick her up.

"Blue, Blue, what's the matter?" Tam shouted. He ran to the cot and stared down at the ugliest baby he had ever seen. It had pointed ears and a tippety nose and a screwed-up cross little face.

"What's happened?" Tam asked. "Where's Blue?"

Mum burst into tears. "Blue's been stolen," she sobbed. "And this little goblin thing's been left in her place."

The Changeling

Tam couldn't take his eyes off the goblin thing. It really was very ugly. But its eyes were as brilliant as blue jewels.

"Sapphires," Tam whispered to Great-grandpa. "Just like those stars we saw."

"What did you say?" Dad asked.

Great-grandpa looked worried.

"The stars were whizzing about last night, weren't they, Great-grandpa? They were deep, deep blue, just like her eyes," said Tam. "And things were flying and fluttering right round the house."

Dad sat down with his head in his hands. "Why didn't you tell me? You silly old man!"

"You were asleep," Great-grandpa muttered. "Anyway, it was nothing, it was nothing."

"What's all that got to do with this ugly thing in Blue's cot?" Mum demanded. "And where is Blue anyway? Where's my baby?"

"Ask Grandpa," Dad said. "He reckons he knows about such things."

Great-grandpa Toby took out his hankie and blew his nose loudly. "Yes, I think I do know. I think this baby is a changeling."

Mum gasped and started crying again.

Tam glared at the baby. She pulled a face at him and he pulled one back, his best one, with his eyes rolled up and his lips curled back like sausages. Instead of crying, the baby giggled and tried to copy him.

"My word," said Great-grandpa, "I've never heard a little baby laugh like that before. It really must be a changeling."

"What's a changeling?" Tam asked.

"A changeling is a fairy child," said Great-grandpa.

"I've heard of this happening," Mum sobbed. "The fairies come and steal a mortal baby and leave a nasty little goblinny thing in its place. I'll never see my baby again!"

The changeling baby stopped pulling faces at Tam and smiled sweetly at him instead. She held out her arms as if she wanted him to pick her up.

"She's really, really ugly," said Tam.

Mum burst into tears again and ran out of the room, and Dad ran after her. Great-grandpa sighed deeply and sat on the chair. The changeling baby gurgled up at Tam.

"She likes you," Great-grandpa said.

"Well I don't like her. I'd rather have Blue back, any day." Tam tried not to catch the goblin-thing's eyes, but she was smiling her crooked smile at him and staring straight at him with her dazzling blue eyes. It made him feel very strange. He could hardly take his eyes off her.

"She's bewitching you," Great-grandpa said.

"No she's not," said Tam. "I'm not going to look at her."

But as soon as he said it, he wanted to look at her again. He went to bed, but all he wanted to do then was to go back to the changeling's room and peer round the door at her. Maybe what Great-grandpa had said was true. Maybe she *had* bewitched him.

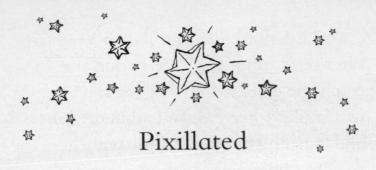

Pixillated

Mum and Dad refused to go near the changeling, but Tam was worried that she might be hungry. He took her some cornflakes and she scowled at him. He took her a bottle of milk and she crossed her eyes.

"She seems all right," said Great-grandpa. "And I don't suppose she'd eat mortal food anyway."

When no one was looking except Tam, the baby stared at a vase of roses till all the flowers flew across the room and landed in her cot.

She gobbled them up greedily,
thorns and all. Then she lay back,
burping loudly.

"Can I carry her into the
garden?" Tam asked Mum.
"I think she likes flowers."

"Just leave her alone," Mum said. "Try
to forget she's here."

But how could they forget? The
changeling shrieked and howled
whenever Tam wasn't in her room.
As soon as he went in, she stopped.
They played the faces game for hours.

"My word, better not go out when
the wind's blowing," Great-grandpa
said. "Soon as it stops, your face will
stick like that."

"It's not my fault," said Tam. "She's making me do it. It's her eyes."

She could do other things with her eyes. She could make all kinds of things happen. When she stared at the cupboard, the doors flew open and all the things in it tumbled out in a mess on the floor. Then she just chuckled and closed her eyes and went to sleep, and nobody but Tam knew it was anything to do with her.

"Did you make that mess?" Mum demanded.

"No, it was the baby," Tam said.

"Don't be silly. Babies can't climb out of their cots and open doors," Mum said. "Not even goblinny things like this one." But she glared at the sleeping baby all the same.

If the baby stared at the clock, the cuckoo popped in and out of its door so wildly that it drove everybody mad with its cuckooing. Nobody saw her do

it except Tam. In
the end Dad took
the clock off the
wall and put it
in the bin.

CUCKOO!

They could hear it cuckooing to itself
out in the yard.

"Cuckoo," sang the goblin baby.
"Cuckoo."

"Shut UP!" shouted Mum.

The baby stared at the window and
the glass shattered like stars.

"My word, this house is pixillated all
right," Great-grandpa chuckled. "I
haven't had such fun for years."

"What's pixillated?" Tam asked.

"Bewitched, enchanted, full of
mischief," Dad said.

Tam leaned over the baby's cot and she blew bubbles at him.

"It's you, isn't it?" Tam whispered. "Pixillating everything, that's what you're doing. I think we should call you Pix."

And the baby smiled at him so sweetly that he actually smiled back. He just couldn't help it.

Great-grandpa came and stood next to him. "My word, you mustn't let her charm you," he said. "Your poor mum's very upset. That baby has to go."

"Go where?"

"Where she belongs," Great-grandpa whispered. "Faery, that's where she comes from. The land of the fairies. Someone's got to take her back there, Tam."

"Only You Can Do It, Tam"

As soon as Mum and Dad had gone out of the room he said it again, only louder, so Tam couldn't pretend he hadn't heard him.

"Someone has to take her to Faery, give her back to the king of the fairies, find Blue and bring her home."

"I suppose so," Tam agreed.

"And there's only you can do it, Tam. My word, you're a brave boy."

"Me? But I can't do that! I'm only nine years old!"

"Exactly," Great-grandpa Toby agreed. "That's why you have to do it."

"But I don't even know how to get there."

"I know the way in," Great-grandpa said. "It's called the green passage."

"How do you know that?"

"Because I once met someone who'd actually been there! He was a very old man, but when he went in, he was just a little boy, like you. And when he came out, he was an old, old man with a beard down to his toes. He'd been there a hundred years, and it just seemed like a day, he said."

"Great-grandpa, I'm not going."

"He told me how to get there, if I ever wanted to go. I never dared. I wasn't brave enough. But I used to go and sit by the green passage and wait in case any fairies came out. I thought I saw the king of the fairies himself, at that very spot, when I was looking through my starburster. Just for a second, I think I saw him, all dressed in green, with hair like dandelion fluff. I think he wanted my starburster, but he wasn't having it. That was ninety years ago." He opened his eyes wide with surprise. "Ninety years!"

"I don't want to go, Great-grandpa."

"You have to take something of your own that's silver and something of your own that's velvet, or you'll never get past the guardian, that's what the old man told me."

Tam sighed with relief. "Well, I can't do it. I haven't got anything of silver, and I haven't got anything of velvet."

Great-grandpa shook his head. "I think you have, Tam. I'm sure you have. And you have to give your favourite thing of all to the king of the fairies."

"My favourite thing? That's not fair!"

"If he gives you Blue back, that's fair, isn't it?"

Tam nodded sadly. He'd almost forgotten about Blue, he'd got so used to Pix.

"You have a think, and I'll have a lie-down," said Great-grandpa. He yawned noisily. "There's something else you have to do, only I can't remember what it is. If you don't do it, you won't come back for a hundred years, like that old man I met. Only I can't remember what it is." He went off to his own room to lie down.

"I really don't want to go!" Tam called after him.

Pix was making her favourite little high-pitched yelping noises. The moon was shining into her cot and she was holding out her hands to it as if she was trying to pull herself up onto its beams. Tam went to his own

bedroom. Mum and Dad would be trying to sleep, he knew, but Pix would be keeping them awake, like she always did. He tried to sleep himself but it was impossible. Her screeches were getting louder. He went back to her room and put his hand through the bars of her cot, and she grabbed hold of his fingers.

"What's the matter, Pix?" he asked. "Do you want to go home?"

As soon as he said that, she stopped crying. And straight away she fell asleep, smiling.

Great-grandpa hurried into the room with his felt slippers flapping and his eyes shining. "I've just remembered what that other thing was! If you don't want to stay in Faery for a hundred years, you have to get there before the stroke of noon on midsummer's day. That's tomorrow, Tam!"

Something of Silver and Something of Velvet

Tam didn't sleep a wink that night. He lifted Pix out of her cot and carried her into his room and put her on his bed. Then he searched through his toys to see if he had something of silver and something of velvet to take. He knew what his favourite thing was, of course. He had no doubt about that, but he wasn't at all happy about giving it to the king of the fairies.

Great-grandpa fussed round the room, clapping his hands and saying, "My word, I can't believe it! Young Tam's going to Faery!"

Tam sat back on his heels. "I don't want to go. But I'm going to rescue Blue," he said, trying to make himself feel brave and happy about it.

"Something velvet and something silver," Great-grandpa reminded him. "Be quick. Oh, I've remembered something else! The silver thing has to be sharp."

"Something silver and sharp," Tam said, gazing round at his pile of things. "Like a . . . "

"Sword!" they both said together, and Pix woke up and stared at the cupboard, and out fell Tam's toy sword. She closed her eyes and chuckled.

"But it isn't sharp at all, because it's only plastic," Tam said. "And it isn't really silver. It's only grey paint."

"Never mind," said Great-grandpa. "It'll do. Something velvet now."

They looked hopelessly round the room.

"Cotton curtains," muttered Great-grandpa. "They're no use. Anyway, they're your mum's. It has to be something of yours."

They stared at the window. Dawn was coming. If they didn't find something soon, it would be too late. Pix started crying, opened her eyes again and glared at the door. And there it was. It just flew off the hook where it always hung, and draped itself round Tam's shoulders.

"My red dressing gown!" he said.
"With its velvet collar!" He stroked the
collar. How he loved the feel of it,
rough one way, smooth the other, just
like a cat's nose.

Great-grandpa took it off Tam's
shoulders and rolled it up. He carried it
downstairs and put it at the bottom of
Pix's pram, then he came back up for

Pix and carried her down. Tam followed with the sword and put it carefully in the pram across Pix's blankets. He couldn't help feeling a surge of excitement as he laid it there. His hand stretched across to touch it.

"Use it carefully," Great-grandpa warned.

"Use it?" said Tam, suddenly scared. "How do I use it?"

"I'm sure the guardian will give you instructions," Great-grandpa said. "There's bound to be Faery rules. They can't just let anyone wander round and do what they like there, can they? Now, Tam, fetch the favourite thing."

Pix chuckled gleefully.

"I wish I didn't have to," said Tam.

"I know," said Great-grandpa.

Tam went back to his room and opened the drawer by the bed. He took out the starburster in its yellow sock. He had a lump in his throat. He felt sadder than he had ever felt before. He carried it downstairs and put it in the pram without saying anything, and Great-grandpa didn't say anything either.

But an amazing thing happened then. The changeling baby stretched out her hands as if she wanted to touch it. Then she nodded her head and smiled, just as if she understood exactly what was going on.

Through the Green Passage

They left the house just as the sun was
pushing above the rooftops. All the air
seemed to be golden that morning.
They didn't wake Mum and Dad,
though Tam was longing to tell them
that he was going to find baby Blue
and bring her home again. But he
knew Mum would worry and fuss and
cry, and that would never do. Tam
would never be able to leave if she did
that. And Dad would insist on coming
with him, and that would never do
either. Dad wasn't a little boy.

So he and Great-grandpa and Pix in
her pram went out of the house as
quietly as they could, down the street

and through the park and across the river and towards the boulders, and at last Great-grandpa stopped.

"This is the place. This is where I met the man with the long white beard that came to his toes."

"But it's just a pile of rocks," Tam said. "This can't be Faery."

Pix was grizzling and grunting, waving her hands about and kicking her feet in the air, rocking the pram so wildly that Tam thought she would fall out of it any minute.

"See that crack between those big pointed rocks?" said Great-grandpa.

Tam nodded.

"That's the green passage. You have to go through there." He bent down and kissed Tam. "My word, you're a brave boy."

Tam's courage was draining away. He didn't feel a bit brave. He wanted to go back home and have a nice breakfast of toast and marmalade instead of going to Faery.

"I don't really want to . . ." he began.

"I'm proud of you," Great-grandpa said.

So Tam gripped the handle of Pix's pram and walked forward towards the crack. He turned round, and Great-grandpa nodded and waved and blew him a kiss. He turned back, and the two great boulders began to roll apart, and the narrow crack opened out to a passage that was as green as summer leaves. Tam took two more steps, then three, then seven, and he was inside the passage. He took two more, and the two great boulders rolled together again like huge doors closing behind him.

Prince Tamlin

It was completely dark now, and completely silent. Tam stood very still, and he and Pix both held their breath.

Something was happening. Tam could hear the sound of shuffling feet, and they were getting closer, closer. They stopped in front of Pix's pram. Now Tam could hear the sound of someone breathing.

Suddenly there was a flash like blue lightning and the passage was lit by a flickering light. Standing in front of Tam was a skinny old man with a green beard and long green hair. He stared at Tam, and Tam stared back at him, too afraid to speak.

The old man pointed a bony finger
at him and said, "Splix."

"Splix?" Tam said
back.

"Who? Splix! Who?"
the man asked,
stamping his foot.

"Who? Tam, I'm Tam.
Are you – are you the
king of the fairies?"

"Sploof!" the skinny
man growled. "Not king!
Look-after. I look after."

"Oh! Are you a sort of
guardian?"

"All of 'em's look
after." The skinny man
swung his arms and the
floor of the passage lit up.
Men were lying all
around them, still as
stones. "Faery soldiers,"
he whispered.

"Are they all dead?" Tam asked.

"Sploof!" the old man said again. "Slumber. Hinx hundert year-in year-out." He held up ten fingers.

"Ten hundred! They've been asleep for ten hundred years. A thousand years?"

Look-after grinned pointed green teeth at him.

"Can't they ever wake up?"

At that moment Pix woke up from her own deep sleep and began to whimper, and at the sound of the baby crying the sleeping soldiers turned over onto their backs.

"Whishht! Wheesh! Sheesh!" Look-after whispered. "Only wake when mortals make war on Faery."

"I'm not making war," Tam promised. "I've just come to see the king of the fairies, and to bring Pix back, and to take Blue back home. Blue's my baby sister, and the fairies stole her, you see, but we want her back."

The guardian peered in the pram. He and Pix pulled faces at each other. He put his hand in the pram and rubbed his fingers up and down her back, and nodded again.

"Don't you like Faery baby?" he asked, puzzled.

Tam stared at Pix. He did like her, he realized. He liked her very much now. She didn't even look very ugly in the flickery green light of the cave.

"Yes, I do like her," he said. "But she's not my sister, you see."

The guardian frowned as if Tam's answer made no sense to him. "Don't *want* her?"

Tam sighed. "I want Blue," he whispered.

Look-after growled and pulled a face at Pix, and she pulled one of her worst ones at him. Then his fingers stole towards the yellow sock, but Tam pulled it away from him.

"You can't have that," he said. "It's a
present for the king of the fairies."

"King?" The guardian glared at Tam.
He thrust his face up to him. "King far
away."

"Great-grandpa says I'll need to take Pix to the king himself." Tam could feel himself shaking now. "Please will you help me?"

The guardian grunted and shook his head. "Only prince see king," he snapped. He walked round Tam, looking him up and down. "Snee snix?" he snarled.

"Snee snix?"

The man stamped his foot. "Snee snix? Sharp silver?"

"Oh yes." Trembling, Tam lifted his sword out of the pram. "But I haven't come to make war with it. It's not sharp. It's only plastic really, and it's grey, not really silver."

But the guardian swished the sword this way and that, until it gleamed as bright as the moon in his hands. He gave it back to Tam. It was a real sword now, sharp and shining like ice, with a blue jewel set deep in the hilt.

"Snee snix splix?" he shouted. "Name him."

"Snee snix splix? Oh, what's the sword called?" Tam closed his eyes. He thought of the name of his street. "Winander," he said.

Look-after grunted. "Vinand'r, Vinand'r. Use Vinand'r well. When you see castle nightmares, snee snix, chop off heads with Vinand'r."

"Chop off their heads? I can't do that!" Tam said. "I can't chop off anyone's head!"

But the guardian just stamped his foot and hissed.

Tam put the sword back in the pram. He tried to wrap it up but the guardian whipped the dressing gown out of his hands and shook it out. It turned into a cloak of deep-red velvet. He grunted with pleasure and swung it round Tam's shoulders, so it fell in soft folds round him. Tam felt magnificent.

The guardian placed the sword
Winander in Tam's belt and stood back
and grinned his green teeth at him.

"Prince Tamlin," he said, bowing his
head. "Welcome to Faery."

Go Wisely, Go Bravely

A voice that was not Look-after's echoed round the passage; a deep, strong, powerful voice. It came from the guardian's mouth, but it was deep and strong and frightening, not at all like his own crackly voice.

Nothing take from Faery, the voice said. *Nor food nor drink take, nor sleep have. Go wisely, go bravely, young Prince.*

Tam looked round, but there was no one to be seen but the green-haired guardian and the sleeping figures.

"How will I find the king?" Tam asked. His voice was shaking a little.

Cross the sapphire lake.

"Sapphire!" Tam said. "Like the stars!"

Do not look at your reflection. You will fall into an enchanted sleep for thousands of years. Remember this . . . remember all these things. The voice was growing fainter.

"And then what do I do, when I've crossed the lake?" Tam asked. There was no answer. "And how do I get across it? And where is it anyway?"

Silence, except for the echo of his own words. *Is it anyway? Anyway? Way?*

The guardian was watching him, arms folded, head on one side, grinning his green toothy grin. "This way, that way," he chuntered in his crotchety old voice. "Kimble."

He clicked his fingers and ambled off, and Tam followed him. It was hard work, pushing the pram over the stony ground, and he didn't want to risk waking the sleepers or making Pix cry. He followed the guardian as carefully as he could. Now he could see daylight ahead of him, and the blue gleam of

water. And on the shore of the sapphire
lake the old man with the green hair
and beard stopped, and disappeared,
just like a candle flame that has
been blown out.

The Sapphire Lake

Tam gazed across the lake, almost
dazzled by its brilliance. It shimmered
ahead of him as wide and as far as his
eyes could see. There was no way
round it or over it; no shore, no bridge.
He felt like crying.

"Now what do I do?" he moaned.

Pix sat up in her pram. "Wish, wish,
a fairy wish," she whispered.

"Pix! Did you really say that? You
can talk! You can sit up already! It's
amazing!"

"Wish, wish, a fairy wish," she
whispered again.

"All right, I wish we had a boat,"
Tam said, and so it happened, just like

that, all in a moment. The pram rolled
into the lake and bobbed there, big
enough for two to sail in. Winander the
sword became a mast, and Tam's red
velvet cloak became the sail. As soon as
he scrambled aboard, the little boat
began to skim across the water.

Pix struggled to sit upright.

"You're too young to sit up," Tam told her, and she gurgled rudely at him. She leaned over the side, pointing down to the water and pulling faces at her reflection.

Tam stared ahead of him. He mustn't look into the lake. Whatever happened he mustn't look.

Pix started shouting and waving her arms about. She could see something in the lake past her own reflection, something wonderful and beautiful that made her face light up with smiles. She twisted her head round to look at Tam, and her eyes were shining. She looked back over the side.

"Ooh, ooh," she crooned. She laughed and sang happily. "Oooh!"

Tam so much wanted to see what she could see. Surely he could look at the lake without seeing his own face in it? Ahead of him he could see only the brilliant glitter of blue light. If he wanted to see anything else, he must look over the side of the boat.

"Oh, oh, oh!" shouted Pix.

And all round Tam hundreds of chattering voices whispered and sang, "Look and see, look and see; there is no such beauty in the mortal world. Look and see."

Tam couldn't resist it any longer. He had to look for himself. He leaned across to see what Pix could see, and at once she twisted round to him, frowning. He heard the voice that had come from the guardian in the green passage echoing round him:

Do not look at your reflection. You will fall into an enchanted sleep for thousands of years. Remember this . . .

Tam pulled himself back quickly, and the whispering voices stopped.

Now the sky and the lake had turned a much deeper blue. It began to rain. The rain turned to hail and crinkled into the bottom of the boat like little blue stones. Tam held out his hand and caught one on his palm. It lay there, not melting but glimmering with fiery blue light.

"Fairy stones. They're jewels," he said. "They must be sapphires! I wish I could show Great-grandpa! He'd know what they are."

The sapphire was beautiful. It glinted and sparkled like a tiny piece of sky.

"Take it," the singing voices chanted. "Have it. It's yours."

"Mum would love these," Tam said to Pix. "I could take her one, just this one." He closed his fingers round the sapphire.

"Yours," the voices sang on. "Yours. Yours."

Pix scrambled round to face Tam, sending the boat-pram rocking danger-ously. Water slapped over the sides. She glared at him until shivers of fear ran up and down his spine.

And the guardian voice came again: *Nothing take from Faery. Nothing take from Faery.*

Tam flung the jewel as far as he could into the lake. It splashed and sank, and sent out a ring of blue ripples that spread like a peacock's tail opening out, wider and wider.

And out of the ripples rose a castle, gleaming white like snow, with golden turrets and towers, and crimson flags flying from all its pinnacles.

The Fairy Castle

The little boat-pram bumped against a
shore of sparkling blue sand. Tam
scrambled out and pulled it out of the
water. Pix gurgled and sang and kicked
her legs and flapped her arms.

"All right, all right, don't be so
impatient," Tam said. "You were just a
tiny baby when we left home. You were
tiny and helpless, and now look at you.
What's happening, Pix?"

He put his cloak round his shoulders
and fixed Winander back into his belt,
slipped the yellow sock into his pocket,
and then bent down to lift Pix out of
the pram. She screeched and pointed at
something behind him, and he turned

round to see three beasts
bearing down on him,
snarling and howling.
They had long heads like
horses and fat bodies like
bulldogs. They had
claws like rusty
nails. They had round red
eyes like flames. They had
teeth like twisted spikes,
and long yellow dripping
tongues. One was red, one
was black, and one was
white. And they thundered
towards the shore.

"Pix frightened," she whimpered.
"I'm a bit scared
myself." Tam looked
round desperately for
somewhere to hide,
but there was nowhere.
Pix whimpered
again.

When you see the castle nightmares, snee snix, came the voice of the guardian.

Tam felt the hilt of the fairy sword against his hand. He drew it out of his belt and swung it round in the air.

Snee snix, chop off heads with Vinand'r.

Wheesh! Wheesh! Winander sang. The nightmare beasts reared up towards Tam. He closed his eyes and gripped the hilt tightly. Wheesh! Wheesh! Wheesh! He chopped off their heads.

Tam opened his eyes and saw the three heads rolling into the lake. The black beast turned into a girl with black hair, the red beast turned into a girl with red hair, and the white beast turned into a girl with white hair. They danced round Tam.

"Thank you, thank you!" they said. "We're free! We're free!"

Tam put Winander back into his belt.

He was still shaking. "What happened?" he asked. "How did you do that?"

The girl with black hair laughed. "*You* did it! You broke the king's spell. You set us free."

"We're fairies again," the red girl sang. They opened out wings like dragon-flies, green and blue and gold, and skimmed round Tam, talking one after the other in a dizzying jumble. "But why did the king turn you into nightmares?" Tam asked. "How could he be so cruel?"

The fairy girls all spoke at once again.

"He sent us to mortal land . . . ."

"Long ago . . ."

"To find what he most desired."

"But we couldn't find it . . ."

"And when we came back without it . . ."

"He was so angry with us . . ."

"That he turned us into nightmares."

"He said only a brave young prince . . ."

"From the land of mortals . . ."

"Could break the spell."

"And that was you," they finished, smiling.

"But I'm only Tam," Tam said.

"Prince Tamlin," Pix reminded him. She flapped her arms like the three fairies, then lost her balance and tumbled backwards. She stuck her thumb in her mouth and scowled.

"And now we're free!" the girls laughed. "Thank you, Prince Tamlin!" They darted away from him, over the sapphire lake. The sound of their laughter floated away like bells.

"I wonder what it was he told them

to find?" Tam said. "The king must be very, very cruel to turn them into nightmares like that. I hope he doesn't do the same to me, Pix. But I'll have to risk it, all the same. I wonder if he's in there?"

He looked up towards the castle. He could see figures on the parapets and leaning out of the towers. Three trumpets were raised – a bronze trumpet, a silver trumpet, and a golden trumpet – and they played a sweet fanfare of welcome that sounded like a forest of birdsong.

Pix raised her arms up to Tam. "Take Pix home."

The Food of Fairies

Sandy-coloured children ran towards
Tam and Pix and led them over six
stepping stones and through the castle
doorway into a courtyard. In the
middle was a fountain that showered a
plume of stars. The stars drifted down
into a pool of silver water. And there
were flowers everywhere, trees filled
with flowers, arches of flowers, lawns of
flowers. The children ran here and there
as if they were showing Pix and Tam
how beautiful it all was.

"Home! Home!" Pix struggled to be
out of Tam's arms and he set her down
gladly. She seemed to be growing
heavier and bigger by the minute. And

he had noticed something strange about her back. Her shoulder blades seemed to be pushing out through the little spotted nightdress that used to belong to Blue. And when she looked up at him, her face was different. She'd lost that hairy, scowly look that she used to have.

She tried to stand up, clinging onto his leg for support, but bumped back down again. She flapped her arms and grumbled. Then she reached out to an archway of roses and clung onto that. Flower petals showered round her and she grabbed them up by the fistful and stuffed them in her mouth.

"Be careful," Tam warned her. "They might be full of grubs."

Pix burped and grinned up at him. Petals were stuck to her wet cheeks and her chin, clinging to her hair. She held out a fistful to him and he shook his head.

Then Tam noticed that the other children were eating flowers too, only more daintily than Pix. They wandered from flower to flower, picking a white petal here and a pink one there and smiling as if they tasted wonderful. It made his stomach growl to watch them. A girl with deep purple-coloured eyes ran over to him, holding out a wooden bowl full of petals.

"Welcome!" she said. "Are you hungry? Nectarine flowers, orange blossom, cherry. Eat, Prince Tamlin." She shook the bowl and the petals turned into gossamer froth that looked like candyfloss and smelled as sweet as strawberries.

A boy came with a crystal goblet of
petals, and when he shook it the petals
turned into sparkling liquid like
lemonade. He held it out to Tam,
nodding at him to take it. Tam was so
hungry now that he felt weak. His
throat was dry with thirst. The first girl
dipped a chocolate twig into the bowl
and put it to his lips. Tam closed his
mouth firmly and shook his head.

"Mustn't!" he said, but oh! he was dizzy with hunger. The children clustered round him with their bowls of delicious-smelling petals. "Just one, just one," they whispered. The purple-eyed girl held out the chocolatey twig again, and now it was so close to his face that he could almost taste the smell. He covered his mouth with his hand, and a voice from nowhere boomed out:

Nor food nor drink take.

Startled, the children sprang away from Tam, looking this way and that to see where the voice was coming from.

"He can see us!" the purple-eyed girl said. "He knows!"

"Who?" Tam asked. "Is it the king?"

And as if he had said the most frightening word that could be imagined, the children dropped their bowls and petals and covered their faces with their hands. And the strange thing was, Tam's hunger and thirst had completely gone.

He turned round to look for Pix, and saw that she had curled herself up on the grass and fallen asleep. Some of the other children were sleeping too, or yawning, or rubbing their eyes. The air was hot and  sweet with the scent of flowers. Tam could hardly keep his eyes open. He was drowsy with the dazzle of sunlight and flowers, and all round him he could hear the steady breathing of sleeping children as one after another they sank to their knees and curled up on the grass. He yawned, and yawned again. "Mustn't sleep, must stay awake," he yawned. His head was so muzzy that he couldn't remember any more why he had to stay awake.

Two of the children came to him and took his hands. They led him to a hammock made of flowers and stitched with daisy chains. He allowed himself to be lifted onto it and rocked gently, backwards and forwards, backwards and forwards. "Sleep, Prince Tamlin. Sleep," they sang, and their voices were so soft and sweet that all he wanted to do was to close his eyes, close his eyes, close his . . . close . . . cl . . .

The Starburster Is Stolen

"No! I mustn't!"

He opened his eyes as wide as he could and stared around.

Nor sleep in Faery have.

"No, I didn't, I wasn't, I wouldn't," Tam stuttered.

But he was the only one to hear the voice this time. All the children were awake now, playing a game of some kind, throwing something in the air, laughing and squealing. Pix was running across the grass towards him, shouting to him to come.

"Look! See!" she called. "Look, Prince Tamlin, look!"

The girl with purple eyes laughed

across at Tam and threw something. She caught the thing that they were playing with and threw it up in the air again, and now Tam could see something yellow slipping away from it and falling to the ground, and the tube that was inside it gleaming as it rose out of her hands.

"Hey! That's my starburster!" Tam shouted. He struggled out of the hammock and ran to a golden-haired boy who had caught the starburster, but as soon as Tam reached him the boy opened out his wings and skimmed away. He passed it to another child, who passed it to another, and Tam ran helplessly from one to the other, jumping and skipping to try to keep up. The purple-eyed girl caught it just as he reached her. She flew up above his head, tossing the kaleidoscope from one hand to the other like a juggling stick, teasing him. Then she flew to a tree by the pool and hung upside down from one of the branches. She dangled there, just out of his reach.

"Please give it back to me!" Tam begged. "I must have it. It's a present for the king of the fairies."

A hush of wonder fell over the children.

"The king!" The girl in the tree gasped. "You're going to see the king!"

"Some fairies stole my baby sister and left Pix instead," Tam said. "So I've brought Pix back, and now I want Blue. And Great-grandpa said I have to give the starburster to the king. Please, please give it back to me."

"You must be very brave, if you're going to see the king," one of the boys said. "Give him his starburster, Elfa."

"Here," Elfa said. "Take it." She let the kaleidoscope slip out of her fingers, but it caught on one of the branches and bounced off as Tam ran to catch it. It fell into the pool with a splash of rainbow light, and sank to the bottom, out of sight.

Tanta

Tam stared at the pool. He couldn't
believe what had happened. Pix put her
hand in his and let out a howl of rage.

"What's happening out here?" A
woman came running towards them,
her golden hair and yellow gown
billowing round her.

"Tanta! Tanta's coming!" Elfa flew
down from her tree and ran to join the
other children. They stood holding
hands, quiet and still. One of the boys
made a bubbling noise as if he were
trying to keep his giggles inside
himself.

The woman stopped and looked
down at Tam. Her hair was as bright

 as sunshine around her face, and her eyes were like silver moons. Tam thought she was more beautiful than anyone he had ever seen.

"Are you the queen of the fairies?" he asked.

The children squawked and giggled, and the woman glared at them until they fell silent again. Then she turned back to Tam.

"I am not the queen of the fairies," she said. "I am Tanta! And who are you?"

"Tam," he whispered, all his courage gone.

"Prince Tamlin," Pix mumbled. She gripped his hand tightly.

Tanta looked down at Pix and plucked at her grubby nightdress. She

turned her round and felt the knobbly
shoulder blades. "I've never seen you
before. You don't belong here."

"I do! I do!" Pix sobbed. She held
out her arms to Tam and he picked her
up. She put her arms round his neck
and he hugged her tightly. His throat
hurt so much that he
could hardly speak.

"I've come all this way to bring Pix back," he said. "I walked through the green passage and I didn't wake the sleepers up. I sailed across the sapphire lake and I didn't take anything. I didn't look at my face in the water. I chopped off the heads of the nightmares and turned them back into fairies. I didn't eat when I was hungry. I didn't drink when I was thirsty. I didn't fall asleep when I was tired. I did all that so I could bring Pix home to Faery and so I could find my baby sister and take her back to Mum. But I have to give my favourite thing to the king, and I haven't got it any more."

Tanta stood with her arms folded, nodding her head. "I believe all that," she said. "You look like a brave boy who could do all that. And what is this favourite thing that you were going to give to the king of the fairies?"

"It's my starburster. It's like magic but it isn't really, Great-grandpa says. It's just clever and beautiful." Tam swallowed hard. "And it's gone."

"Gone where?"

Tam couldn't say any more. It was all too much. He stared at the pool and tears trickled down his cheeks. The fairy children gasped in horror and clustered round him, stroking his cheeks, patting him, whispering, "Don't break, Prince Tamlin. Don't break."

"Now stop that," said Tanta. "It's too sad."

Then she did an amazing thing. She stood on the edge of the pool and dived into it, and as she dived she turned into a golden fish. Seconds later she came up out of the pool in a ring of ripples and leaped into the air like a salmon. She twisted round and became herself again, standing next to Tam, completely dry. She held the starburster in her hands.

"Can I look?" she asked.

Tam nodded. He was too surprised to speak. He had actually seen fairy magic. Wait till I tell Great-grandpa! he thought.

Tanta lifted up the kaleidoscope and peered through it. She twisted it this way and that, peering at the water and the fountain and the sky and the flowers, and it seemed as if she never wanted to stop looking through it. "Man magic!" she said softly. "How wonderful it is."

She gave it back to Tam at last and watched how carefully he snuggled it into the yellow sock. He put it into his pocket and kept his hand over it, just in case.

"Come with me to the baby glade," Tanta said. "We'll see if we can find your sister."

The Baby Glade

Tanta led Tam and Pix to a shady orchard. Dabs of sunlight filtered through the leaves of fruit trees. In the cool shadows cradles were being rocked by tall elves. They all looked alike, with pointed ears and green eyes and flowing white hair.

Most of the babies were sleeping. Some were holding their hands up towards the trees, as if they wanted to catch the dapples of sunlight and shadows. Some were playing with their toes. They made the little gurgling sounds that Pix loved to make. Some bigger babies were sitting on the grass, picking tiny flowers and sucking the

petals. From time to time they flapped their arms up and down.

A very few of them had tiny buds of feathers sprouting from their shoulder blades. And there were about six who had fully grown wings that opened and shut, opened and shut like the wings of butterflies. Pix pointed to them and waved her arms up and down. They stood on the tips of their toes and rose in the air, just about leaving the ground, and landed again with a bump. They laughed with excitement.

"Very good, flightlings," Tanta said as she passed them. "Soon you'll be flying. Then you won't be in the baby glade any more."

The flightlings smiled proudly at each other.

"Why haven't you got wings?" Tam asked Tanta shyly.

"Grown-ups don't have wings. We don't need them. I lost mine a long time ago."

"Don't you mind?" Tam looked back to the children by the fountain, swooping and diving in the air like birds. How he would love to be able to do that.

✿ 84 ✿

"Mind?" Tanta put her head to one side and thought. "Nobody really minds growing up, Prince Tamlin. Though I must say, I loved my wings. They were golden. But as soon as I lost them, I was able to shape-change, and that's very useful."

"Is that how you turned into a salmon? What else can you do?"

"That's my secret," Tanta said. "And I never, never shape-change unless it's really important. If I did it just for fun the king would make me stay that shape for ever."

"Like pulling faces? Great-grandpa says that if the wind changes when I'm pulling a face, I'll stay like that."

"Exactly. He sounds very wise, your great-grandpa. Now, have a look in the cradles and see if you can find your sister. They don't have wing-stumps when they're very small, so I really wouldn't know a fairy baby from a mortal baby."

"Mortal babies are prettier," Tam wanted to say, but didn't. He looked at Pix. She really was very pretty now she was back in Faery. Even Mum would like her.

He went from cradle to cradle and peered inside every one. He didn't have to look for wing-stubs to know that they were all fairies. Blue definitely wasn't there. When he came to the last cradle he felt like crying again.

"Are there any more baby glades?" he pleaded. "She must be somewhere else."

Tanta shook her head. "All the babies are brought here as soon as they're born, and they stay with me till they can fly. I'm sorry, Prince Tamlin. There are no more babies in the whole of Faery."

Keekwee Baba

One of the elves had been holding Pix while Tam looked into the cradles. He came over now and said something in a strange language to Tanta.

"Keekwee baba?"

"Keekwee baba?" Tanta looked shocked. The elf pulled his ears and rocked his head from side to side.

Tanta turned back to Tam. "Morva says there is one more baby in Faery. But she's not your sister. She can't be."

Tam's heart rose. There was a chance; surely there was a chance. "Can I see her?"

"She's far away from here," Tanta said. "And she belongs to Keekwee.

That's what the elves call the king and queen. You're not going to tell me that the queen would steal a human baby and bring her up as a fairy, are you?" She stood with her hands on her hips, glaring down at Tam. "If anyone even dared to suggest it the king would turn them into tadpoles, or something much worse."

But Tam was already moving away. "Tell me where they live. I'm going to have a look."

"You'll never find your way there on your own," Tanta called after him. "They're in their secret tower. No one is allowed to go there unless they're sent for. Hardly anyone in Faery knows the way there. Even I don't."

The elf pulled his ears again and spoke in his quick, light voice. "Emba fost ni glaz pintos."

"Morva says it's somewhere over there, past the emerald forest, up in the crystal mountains." Tanta pointed to shimmering icy mountains in the distance. "That's all he knows."

"I'll find it," said Tam. He took Pix out of the elf's arms. "I'll get there."

"Don't even try," Tanta insisted. "It's too far for you to walk, Prince Tamlin. You're only a child."

"It doesn't matter. I'll get there, however long it takes. I'm not going home without Blue," Tam said. He was scared and worried and excited, all at the same time. "Come on, Pix."

He started off out of the baby glade again, in the direction of the distant crystal mountains. They seemed so far away, and so high, and so icy, that he had no idea how he was going to do it. And when he did get to the secret tower, he had the wicked king of the fairies to face.

"It seems so impossible," he whispered to Pix. "But we've got to do it."

And Pix whispered back, "Wish, wish, a fairy wish."

"A fairy wish!" sighed Tam. "How I wish a fairy would help me!"

Pix squirmed in his arms, pointing excitedly over his shoulder. Tam turned round, and saw the most wonderful thing. Tanta had gone, and a horse was trotting towards them; a beautiful white horse with silver eyes like moons and a long flowing golden mane.

"Tanta?" Tam said.

The horse stopped by him. "Yes," she said, in a snorty, horsey voice.

The elf ran up to him and took Pix out of his arms, and Tam climbed onto Tanta's back. They set off, with Morva running in front of them, leading the way to the secret tower.

The Secret Tower

It was a long way. The emerald forest
was deep and dark. The trees stretched
out long fingers and pulled Tam
forwards and backwards and sideways
and nearly upside down. They plucked
at his cloak, they scratched his cheeks,
they pulled his hair. He could hear Pix
whimpering with fright. Morva held
her up to Tam and he leaned down
and took her. The little elf tumbled
head over heels with relief. Pix was
getting much too heavy to be carried.

Tam clicked his tongue. "On, on,
Tanta," he urged. He rode with one
arm round Pix, and his free hand
grasping Tanta's mane, while Morva

ran ahead. It was better that way, and it was comforting for Tam to have Pix with him. She chuntered happily into his ear, chewing it from time to time.

When they came out of the emerald forest at last, the crystal mountains reared above them, shiny and smooth as glass, cold as ice. Morva took Pix for a while so Tam could rest his arms, then passed her back as they started to climb the mountain. Tanta's hooves slipped and slithered. Tam was jerked backwards and forwards, but he clung onto Pix and he hung onto the golden mane. He clicked his tongue.

"On, on, Tanta," he urged.

And at last they could see the tower, as white as ice. Wispy clouds like veils swirled round it. Huge white birds with trailing feathers and piercing golden eyes swooped in and out of the mist.

"Keekwee tower!" Morva squatted on the ground with his legs crossed. He was trembling uncontrollably. He put his hands over his eyes as if he were trying to hide.

Tanta stopped. "I daren't go any further, Prince Tamlin," she said. "If the king sees me he'll make me stay a horse for ever. He might even turn me into a nightmare."

Tam slid down from her back, still clutching Pix, who was fast asleep. "Thank you for bringing me," he said. He couldn't take his eyes off the tower.

"Goodbye, Prince Tamlin. Good luck," Tanta said.

The last slope leading up to the tower was steep and slippery. Tam walked more and more slowly. He was shaking, but he didn't know whether it was with fear or tiredness. A flight of glass steps led up to the entrance, but he could hardly lift his legs to climb them. He gazed up at the tower in despair.

"I mustn't give up now, I mustn't give up now," he kept saying to himself. He put Pix down and she woke up immediately. She tried to stand up, wriggling her back from time to time as though her shoulders were itchy. There was a sudden tearing sound, and her grubby nightie ripped in two places. The feathery tips of little wings poked through the holes.

"Pix! You're nearly a flightling!" Tam said.

"I know! I know!" She beamed up at him. "Can you see them? Can you see my wings?" Her tiny feathery wings opened up like daisies, then closed again.

But she still couldn't walk, and she still couldn't fly. Tam lifted her up again and staggered up the last few steps with her. He put her down by the amber door at the entrance to the tower.

"I can't carry you any further," he panted. "You stay there and practise opening your wings. I'm going in on my own."

Blue Is Found

The inside of the tower was filled with
golden light. Someone was singing a
lullaby in a low, rich, beautiful voice
that made Tam long to lie down and
go to sleep.

"But I mustn't," he told himself. "I
mustn't go to sleep. I must find Blue. I
must find Blue."

The singing was coming from the
centre of the golden light. It nearly
dazzled him, but he shielded his eyes
with his hand and crept as close as he
dared. And it was as if he were walking
through a wall of light, because inside
all the brightness everything was dim
and soft, like the glow of candles. A

woman with long dark hair the colour
of damsons was lying in a hammock
made of silvery spider webs. She wore a
skirt of grass-green silk, and yellow
satin shoes. She had a sleeping baby in
her arms and she was singing to it.

She seemed not to know that Tam was there. He tiptoed closer still, and closer. He was sure — he was so sure — that the baby was Blue.

The woman's singing grew fainter and slower. Tam could see that she was falling asleep. At last the singing stopped. The rocking stopped. The hammock stopped swinging. The fairy woman was fast asleep. Tam took a deep, slow breath and stepped forward. One pace. Two paces. Three paces. So near, and now he could see the baby's face. It *was*. It was Blue.

Tam reached forward and touched the baby's cheek, very gently. She opened her eyes at once and stared at him with wonder. Then he put his hands under her and lifted her out of the fairy queen's arms.

"Stop!" A voice like thunder echoed round the tower. Sapphire-blue lights flashed around Tam. He clutched Blue

close to him and tried to run through
the outer ring of dazzling light towards
the amber
door. Now he
could see that
the blue lights
were spiders,
dipping and
bobbing down
towards him on
silky strands.

They danced round him, spinning their
threads until they wrapped him so
tightly that he couldn't move his arms
or his legs.

And there in front of him, brighter
than any light, was the king of the
fairies. He was dressed in a long tunic
of white linen. He had wild silver hair
like a crown of dandelion fluff, and his
eyes were golden and piercing. And he
was furious. He raised both his fists
above his head and strode towards
Tam.

"How dare you come to Faery,
mortal boy?" the king roared. "How
dare you enter my secret tower? And
how dare you steal my baby
daughter?"

The King of the Fairies

Tam struggled helplessly in his gossamer bindings. If only he could get his right hand free, he could pull his sword Winander out of his belt and chop through the spider strands. But there was nothing he could do to free himself.

The queen was awake now. She came running to stand at the king's side. She stared at Tam.

"He's only a child," she said. "Don't bind him so tight."

The king snapped his fingers and the web bindings fell away from Tam as if they were strands of hair. The queen tried to take Blue out of Tam's arms but he clung tightly to the baby. She snuffled and chuckled into his ear.

"Don't try to run away with her," the king said, "or I will turn you to stone for ever." He smiled at the queen. "He would make a pretty statue for your rose garden."

"Who are you, and what are you doing here?" the queen asked Tam.

"And don't lie," the king said. "Fairies hate lies! I can read lies, and I can read the truth. If you lie, my spiders will bind you again." The spiders bobbed round Tam on their long threads. Their jewel eyes glistened.

"I'm Tam. The fairies call me Prince Tamlin." His voice was tiny and shaky, but as soon as he spoke, the spiders ate up their threads and bobbed back up towards the hazy ceiling of the tower.

"Prince Tamlin," the king repeated, with a mocking smile. "Well, you have your velvet cloak and your silver sword. I suppose you must be a prince. And what are you doing here, Prince Tamlin?"

Tam breathed deeply to find the courage to speak again. "You stole Blue away from us, but we want her back."

"How dare you accuse us of stealing!" the king roared.

"Fairies never steal," screamed the queen into Tam's face. "Fairies take what they want, but we always leave a gift behind."

"What we want, we always get," said the king. "Always. But our servants will have left you something in exchange." He stamped his foot. "We never steal."

Tam shouted back at him, "But you never even asked us! You're wicked and cruel!" He closed his eyes. *Now* what had he done? "Why did you take our baby?" he whispered.

The queen stroked Blue's hand, and her voice became soft and sweet again. "I like mortal babies. My servants did well to choose this one. She will have a beautiful life here with us." She peered at Tam. "You could stay too."

Tam shook his head fiercely. He was too scared to speak now. He looked up at the spiders, and they peered down at him with eyes like black jet. The king walked round and round him in silence.

"I can see he's a brave boy," he said at last. "But he won't do for Faery." He snapped his fingers in Tam's face. "Go away. Go home. I won't punish you for coming. Leave the baby, and go home safely to the land of mortals."

"No," said Tam. He could feel Blue's soft breath against his cheek. "I came all this way. I came through the green passage without waking the sleepers up. I crossed the sapphire lake and I didn't look into it. I chopped off the heads of the nightmares. I did all these things so I could find Blue again and take her home. And I won't go home without her. I won't. I won't."

Again the queen tried to take Blue out of his arms, and again Blue and Tam clung to each other.

"I brought the fairy baby with me," Tam said. "She's called Pix. She can talk already. She's prettier than she used to be. She's very nice, but we didn't want her. We wanted our own baby. And I carried her most of the way here because she can't walk and she can't fly. She's very heavy, but I didn't drop her and I didn't leave her behind."

"And tell me," said the king suddenly. "How did you find my secret tower? How did you get here?"

Tam hesitated. The spiders began to bob down towards him again.

"I came through the emerald forest and over the crystal mountains," he said.

"On your own?" The king's golden eyes seemed to look right into Tam's mind.

Tam was cold with fear. If he lied, then the spiders would spin their threads round him again and he would never be free; he would never go home. But if he told the truth, Tanta and Morva would be punished. They would be turned into nightmares. He had no idea what to say.

The Starburster

"Whee! Look at Pix!" There
was a sudden excited shout and a
bundle of feathers shot through the
amber doorway and came hurtling into
the tower. "Pix can fly!" she shouted,
swooping round them, her starry wings
spangling in the light. "Whee!"

The king and queen ducked as she
whizzed over their heads. She skidded
to a halt at their feet, stray feathers
floating round her, and beamed up at
Tam. She closed her wings and gasped
for breath. "I'm a real fairy now!"

She fluttered her wings open and
took off again, just missing the king.
The queen laughed and caught her.

"Not so fast!" she said. "You'll break your wings if you go as fast as that!" Pix landed again. "I'll show you," the queen said. She lifted her arms as if they were wings and moved them slowly and gracefully up and down. "Like this."

"This is Pix," Tam said. "Your servants left her behind in exchange for Blue. *She* can be your daughter."

"Yes, please!" said Pix. She smiled her best smile and fluttered her wings.

"She's very pretty," the queen said.

"And her wings are beautiful," the king said.

It was then that Tam knew that it was quite safe for him to put Blue down and rest his arms for a bit. Nobody was going to snatch her away. The king and queen were far too busy admiring Pix's starry wings. And just as he put Blue down in the hammock, Pix flew over to him and whispered, "Don't forget the special thing!" She whizzed away again, humming happily.

"The special thing! I nearly forgot!" Tam ran to the king. "I've brought you something in exchange for Blue! I've brought you a present," he said. He put his hand in his pocket and pulled out Great-grandpa's yellow sock.

"Thank you," said the king, not taking his eyes off Pix.

"It's not the sock," Tam explained. "It's what's inside it that's special."

"Thank you," the king said again. He put his hand inside the sock and pulled out the kaleidoscope. His face lit up with surprise and pleasure. "I've seen one of these before!" he shouted. "Look! Look at my present! It's a . . . it's a . . ."

"It's a starburster," Tam said. "At least, that's what Great-grandpa calls it. You put it up to your eye and look through it."

"And you twist it this way, and you twist it that way," the king said,

looking through it.

"The other end," Tam said, and turned it the right way round for him.

"Oh, man magic!" the king breathed, peering through the kaleidoscope. He danced on the tips of his toes with excitement. "Nothing in Faery is as wonderful as this. Oh, I've always wanted one of these." He walked around with it, peering at everything — at his feet, at the queen, at Pix's wings, at his spiders — and every new thing he looked at made him gasp and laugh out loud. "My word!" he said.

"That's what Great-grandpa says."

"I saw a little boy looking through one of these once," the king said, still not taking the kaleidoscope away from his eye. "It was in mortal land, and it was just outside the green passage. He was looking through a . . . a starburster just like this and he kept saying, *My word! My word!* Oh, I so much wanted to see what he could see! I looked through the other end and he looked straight at me! And he shouted out loud, *My word! A fairy!*"

Tam felt a great bubble of excitement inside him. "I know who it was! Was it about ninety years ago?"

"I think it was yesterday," the king said. He took the kaleidoscope away from his eye for just a second. "But time is different in Faery. Actually, Prince Tamlin, he looked a bit like you."

Home

The king and queen and Pix spent a long time looking through the kaleidoscope and laughing and exclaiming, "My word!" at every new thing they saw. Tam rocked Blue in the hammock, watching them, and as soon as she woke up he lifted her out and said, "If you don't mind, I think we'd better go now."

"Of course," said the king. He looked surprised, as if he had forgotten all about Tam. "Any time. I'll send for someone to show you the way. They'll be at the bottom of the glass steps."

"Thank you for bringing our fairy child back," said the queen. "Your sister is very nice, but I really think I like Pix better."

Pix flew up to Tam. She landed daintily and smiled up at him. "Goodbye, Prince Tamlin. Thank you for looking after me." She fluttered her wings for him.

"It's all right, Pix," he said. His voice was husky. "Take care now." He couldn't bring himself to say goodbye, but walked slowly through the dazzling light and out through the amber archway.

And there, waiting for him at the bottom of the glass steps, were a white horse with a long flowing golden mane and silver eyes, and an elf with green hair and pointed ears.

"Tanta and Morva! You're still here!" Tam ran down the steps. Morva helped him onto Tanta's back and handed Blue back up to him, and they were off, galloping like the wind, over the crystal mountains, through the emerald forest, and they came to the white castle.

"Off you get," said Tanta. "We can't take you any further."

Tam handed Blue down to Morva and slid off Tanta's back, and when he turned round the horse had gone, and there was golden-haired Tanta again, smiling at him and rocking Blue in her arms.

"Mortal babies are very beautiful!" she sighed. "No wonder the king and queen wanted one. And no wonder your mother wants her back. There's your boat, waiting for you."

Sure enough, there was the little pram-boat on the blue sand. Morva helped Tam to push it into the water. He bowed to Tam and then clasped both his hands in his own.

"Far good Tamlinkee," he said. "Far good baba."

"Far good Morva," said Tam. He climbed into the boat.

Tanta handed Blue down to Tam and pushed the boat gently away from the shore. She clapped her hands.

"Goodbye, Prince Tamlin," she called. "Goodbye, Baby Blue."

The pram-boat scudded across the sapphire lake with Winander for a mast and the velvet cloak for a sail, and in no time at all they had reached the other side. Tam pulled it out of the water and it became a pram again.

"Nearly there, Baby Blue," he said, and she gurgled sleepily at him. He trundled her over the rocky ground into the dark tunnel. A flickering light came towards him. Now he could see old Look-after, with the green hair and the long green beard. The old elf came straight up to the pram and peered inside. He grinned his green toothy grin, and pointed a bony finger at Blue. She curled her own fingers round it and hiccuped.

"Splix?" Look-after asked.

"Splix? Oh, her name! She's called Blue. My baby sister Blue," Tam said proudly.

"Baba satta Blue," said Look-after softly.

Then he jerked his head and led Tam past the sleeping guardians to the dark cave. He bowed.

"Goodbye, Prince Tamlin!"

Tam paused for a moment. He could still hear Pix's voice, as clear as anything, laughing and singing far away. He could hear the queen and king of the fairies, he could hear Elfa and the other sandy-coloured children, and Tanta and Morva, and then all the voices faded away. Tam felt his cloak slipping away from his shoulders and Winander sliding out of his belt. He looked down and saw his dressing-gown and plastic toy sword on the stony ground, and bent down to pick them up. And just as he put them at the bottom of Blue's pram two huge boulders at the end of the cave rolled apart, and daylight flooded through.

He pushed the pram down the green passage. The boulders rolled to behind him, and there sitting on the grass in front of him were Mum and Dad and Great-grandpa, eating sandwiches and drinking lemonade.

"My word," said Great-grandpa. "It's our Tam."

"Just in time for the picnic," said Dad.

And Tam lifted Blue out of the pram and put her, safe and sound, into Mum's arms.

THE
HUMMING
MACHINE

BERLIE DOHERTY

Illustrated by Lesley Harker

For Tommy

Contents

This is what happened last time:

Great-grandpa Toby gave Tam a present. It was a kaleidoscope, but they called it a starburster. They could see wonderful things through it. One day, Tam's baby sister Blue was stolen by fairies, who left ugly goblinny Pix in her place. Tam had to take Pix back and find Blue again, and he had to give the king of the fairies his starburster.

Stop That Noise

Tam was dreaming about a wonderful little tube called a starburster. When he looked through it he saw the most gorgeous shapes and colours. He had dreamed the same thing every night since midsummer's day, and he always enjoyed the dream till he got to the last bit, when he had to give the starburster away. But tonight something woke him up before he got to that bit.

Tam sat up in bed with a start. There was a terrible noise coming from somewhere. It sounded like a tin can full of bees, all buzzing at once. Or a motorbike in the bath. Or a piano being dropped downstairs – *buzz thump clang wuzz ding fuzz.*

It was awful, and it was coming from Great-grandpa Toby's room. Tam jumped out of bed and ran to see what was happening. Everyone was awake now. Mum was shouting, Baby Blue was screaming, and Dad was hammering on Great-grandpa Toby's door.

"Stop that noise!" everyone shouted – except for Blue, who stopped screaming, took a deep breath and screamed again, only louder.

The noise from Great-grandpa's room grew wilder and buzzier, and much worse. And now there was a kind of thumping sound too. The floor was shaking and creaking.

"You're a noisy old nuisance!" shouted Dad. "I wish you'd go and live somewhere else." He stormed off back to bed.

But the buzzing and thudding and creaking didn't stop.

Tam pushed open the door and peered in.

Great-grandpa Toby was dressed in his red stripy pyjamas. He was bouncing round the room, up and down, one step, two steps, kick, hop, jump. He was holding both his hands up to his mouth as if he was eating a sandwich. And the buzzy tin can motorbike piano noise was coming from him!

"How do you do that?" Tam shouted. And again, "How do you do it?"

But Great-grandpa Toby had his eyes closed and couldn't see Tam. The noise he was making was so loud that he couldn't hear him. And he was jumping and kicking and hopping so wildly that it was impossible to get anywhere near. It was a terrible shindig he was making.

At last he stopped. He sank down on the edge of his bed with a sigh like a vacuum cleaner that's just been switched off. His room was filled with silence. Beautiful, white, cool silence.

But Tam was still shouting, "*How do you do that?*"

He noticed that the noise had stopped.

"Great-grandpa," he whispered. "Tell me."

Great-grandpa opened his eyes and beamed at Tam. "My word, that was fun!" he said. "Look, Tam, isn't it beautiful!" He opened his hands and showed Tam a shiny silver mouth organ. "I bought it today. It's a humming machine."

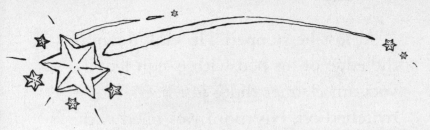

The Humming Machine

All next day Great-grandpa and Tam took it in turns to play the humming machine. Great-grandpa had to show Tam how to do it.

"Put it against your lips. Now, you suck in to make one sound, and you blow out to make another. And you slide it from side to side to do the do-ray-mi's. It's easy. As easy as breathing. As easy as humming a tune."

It made Tam's teeth feel tingly and his lips feel rubbery, and it tasted horrible, like the taste you get when you've just lost a tooth. But the noise it made inside his head was really exciting.

Dad said he'd had enough of it and was glad he was out at work all day. Mum said it gave her a headache, and she put the radio on really loud to drown out the noise. Baby Blue hated the sound at first, but she got used to it and started to gurgle and giggle whenever she heard it.

After a bit, Great-grandpa stopped sounding like a singing robot and started to be able to play real tunes. Mum even sang along with him sometimes, when she wasn't thinking.

"My word," said Great-grandpa. His lips were red with so much blowing and sucking, as if he'd been eating strawberries. "I've lived for ninety years and I've never played a humming machine before."

"You might be ninety years old," said Mum, "but you're behaving like a nine-year-old. Put that harmonica away and eat your lunch."

But as soon as Great-grandpa put it down, Tam picked it up. He got used to the tingly teeth and the wubbly lips. He got used to the tangy taste. He loved it as much as Great-grandpa did. He loved the little box it lived in when it wasn't being played at all. It had a lid that snapped shut like a crocodile's mouth, and inside it was lined with soft green velvet.

"It's the best thing ever!" he said.

"My word," said Great-grandpa Toby. "It's nearly as good as the starburster."

And Tam went quiet and sad, because really nothing, nothing in the world, was as good as his starburster. And he'd given that to the king of the fairies. He'd had the most exciting adventure of his life when he had gone to Faery to rescue Blue – but oh! how he missed his wonderful starburster!

When he went to bed that night he
was still a little bit sad. He couldn't
sleep. He was still awake when Mum
and Dad went to bed. He knew Great-
grandpa was still awake too, because he
could hear him playing his humming
machine. It wasn't his usual bright and
breezy shindig of a tune. He was
playing quietly so he wouldn't disturb
anyone, and the tune was as soft and
sad and sweet as drops of rain. Tam lay
in bed listening to it and watching how
the moon filled his room with blue
light.

Suddenly he jumped out of bed and
ran to the window.

The moon was blue!

"Remember the Sapphire Stars?"

Tam ran straight to Great-grandpa's room. He gave him such a fright that Great-grandpa nearly swallowed his humming machine.

"Great-grandpa, look! Look at the sky!" Tam shouted.

"My word!" said Great-grandpa, pulling back his curtains. "I've never seen anything like this, Tam. It's the rarest thing you can have, a blue moon. Once in a blue moon, anything can happen. Fancy, I've lived all these years and this is the first time I've seen a blue moon."

"And look at the stars! They're blue as well! And they're dancing!"

It was true. The stars were dancing
and swarming in the sky as if they were
brilliant blue bees.

"Remember the sapphire stars?" Great-grandpa asked softly.

"Of course I do," said Tam. "We saw them the night Blue was stolen by the fairies."

They looked at each other. "It had better not happen again!" they both said at the same time.

They ran into Blue's room. It was bathed in sapphire light. But Blue was still there in her cot, safe and sound. She opened her eyes sleepily and smiled at them.

"Thank goodness you're safe!" said Tam. He lifted her out of her cot with her blanket still wrapped round her to keep her warm, and hugged her tight.

"The fairies are coming, Blue. But don't
be frightened. We won't let them steal
you this time. Will we, Great-grandpa?"
He heard a slight whirring sound,
and turned round quickly.

Great-grandpa Toby had gone.

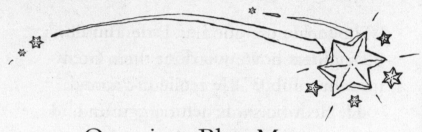

Once in a Blue Moon

Standing just where Great-grandpa
Toby had been was a little girl with
golden-sandy-coloured skin and bright
yellow hair. She smiled proudly at Tam.

"I did it! My first job, and I got it
right, Tam."

"Who are you?" Tam asked.

The little girl sighed. "Don't you
remember me? Don't you remember me
at all?" She rolled her lips back and
pulled the ugliest, goblinniest face you
can imagine, and then smiled sweetly at
Tam again.

"You're Pix!" Tam gasped. "Pix,
you've come back! I never thought I'd
see you again!" His voice sounded

strange. He coughed and tried again.
"But what have you done with Great-
grandpa Toby?" He really did sound
odd. His voice was getting gruffer and
deeper.

Pix didn't seem to notice. "The king
of the fairies wanted to see him," she
said. "So we've – well, we've just
whisked him off to Faery. He'll be fine.
Guess what! I flew here all on my own,
Tam." She skipped round so he could
see how her shimmery wings were
folded neatly across her back.

"Great-grandpa's gone to Faery?" Tam repeated in his strange new voice. He cleared his throat to try to make the gruffness go away, but it didn't help. "But I thought only a nine-year-old boy could go there."

"Exactly," said Pix. She stopped skipping about. "I had to do a little switching job. It's worked so well! I'm so clever! No one will know the difference."

"Pix! What have you done?" With horror, Tam realized why his voice had grown so deep. He felt his chin. It was prickly with whiskers! And when he lowered Blue back into her cot, he could see that his hands were bumpy and spotty, just like Great-grandpa Toby's.

"Oh no!" His voice was growly with tears. "I know what you've done. You've turned Great-grandpa into a nine-year-old boy, and you've turned me into an old man! I'm my own great-grandpa!"

"Don't break, Tam," Pix said anxiously. "Please don't break. You're a very nice old man."

"But I don't want to be an old man.

I won't be able to play football, or ride my bike! And what will they say when I go to school? My friends will all laugh at me! They won't even know me!"

"It'll be all right, Tam. And think what a nice time your great-grandpa's having in Faery."

Tam stopped crying. "I don't believe he's gone to Faery. When I went there I had to take something silver and something velvet with me. What about those? He hasn't got anything like that."

"Oh yes he has," said Pix happily. She put her hands to her mouth and made a buzzing noise.

"His humming machine," Tam sighed. "And its velvet box. So it's true, he *has* gone, and I'll never be a young boy again." His voice was wobbling. Then he brightened up again. "Ah, I know he hasn't really gone to Faery! You can only go there on the stroke of noon on midsummer's day – and it's winter now. Midsummer's day was ages ago!"

He felt happier now. At least if Great-grandpa was tucked up in bed or hiding somewhere, there was a chance that Pix might change them back again before it was too late. But she just smiled her sweetest smile at him and hopped onto the windowsill.

"Once in a blue moon, anything can happen," she said. "Remember?"

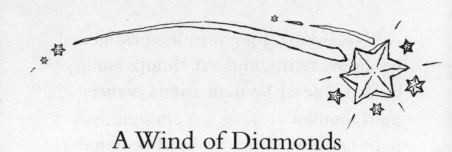

A Wind of Diamonds

"I thought you were nice, Pix. I thought you were my friend," Tam said. He was beginning to feel angry. He looked down at his wrinkled hands. "Just look what you've done to me."

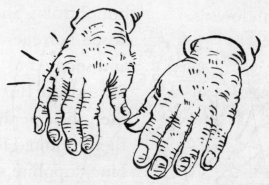

Pix stopped her ecstatic whizzing round the room and stared at Tam. "Don't you like being a very old man?" she asked, surprised.

"No, I don't. I want to be myself again. Now. If you don't change me back, I'll never be your friend again," Tam shouted.

In the next room, his mother called back sleepily, "All right, Grandpa?"

"See! Even Mum thinks I sound like him," Tam whispered. "Please! I love Great-grandpa Toby. But I don't want to be him. Please make me nine again."

Pix plucked a rose from the vase on the windowsill and chewed the petals

thoughtfully. She closed her eyes and seemed to fall fast asleep. But then she opened them again. Her blue, sapphire eyes stared at Tam as if she could see right through him.

He felt a strange sensation, as if his skin was being wound up tight, and a prickly, itchy feeling in his chin. He touched his face nervously. It was smooth once more. He looked down at his hands. They were soft and young. Tam's hands.

"My word," a deep voice came from Blue's cot. "I do feel strange."

Tam stared into the cot. "Now you've turned *Blue* into Great-grandpa!" he said. "Look at her whiskery face! What kind of a fairy are you?"

"Yes, what's going on?" grumbled Blue.

"Oops!" said Pix. "Not quite right!"
Tam peered anxiously at his baby
sister with her crumpled face and
watery eyes. "What's Mum going to
say?" he asked. "Pix, you're going to
have to do something about this."

"All right, all right. I'm only a
beginner, you know." She blew gently
through the bars of the baby's cot, and
something sparkled in the pale blue
moonlight, drifting down like tiny flakes
of snow.

"Aboo. Abababoo," gurgled Blue happily. She was a baby again. She stuck her thumb in her mouth and went to sleep. Tam looked down and checked his hands, just to make sure he was still a boy.

Pix sighed with relief. "Just a little joke! Aren't we having fun! But someone's going to have to be an old man, or my magic won't work. Let's see now!"

She gazed round Blue's room, and then stared at a big fluffy teddy bear that was perched on a shelf.

"Aha!" she said, tapping Teddy's threadbare paw.

"My word!" the teddy bear growled.

"That'll do," Pix said. "I don't think I can manage more than that. Oh but Tam, look at the moon. It's fading."

It was true. The stars were still and silver again. The moon was slipping down behind the rooftops, just the palest of blues.

"Get your silver and velvet quickly!" Pix said.

"Why?"

"I was having such a good time, I nearly forgot. The king wants to see you too. And I'm allowed to fly you to Faery all by myself, because we're friends. We are, aren't we?" she added anxiously. "Quick, before the moon turns white, or we'll never make it."

Tam felt a tingly rush of excitement and fear. Faery again! Last time it had been full of danger and adventure. He had seen so many wonderful things, but now it all felt as if it had been a fantastic dream. Would he really dare to go again? But it looked as if he would be going anyway, whether he wanted to or not, the way Pix rushed him about.

They ran into Tam's room and found his red dressing gown with its furry velvet collar, and then the plastic sword that he and Dad had painted grey when he was about seven. Tam remembered how the green-toothed guardian of Faery had turned his dressing gown into a cloak, and his plastic toy into a real flashing silver sword. He tried to remember the name he had given it. Winander – that was it, after the name of his road. And the guardian had changed it to a fairy name. Vinand'r.

"I won't have to use it again, will I?" he asked, worrying again. "I had to chop off the nightmares' heads with it last time."

"If you don't hurry up, *I'll* be turned into a nightmare," Pix said. "We're ready now, surely."

"Oh, wait a minute. I've just remembered something." Tam tiptoed into Blue's room and planted a kiss softly on her head, very careful not to wake her up.

"Bye, Baby Blue," he whispered. "I don't know when I'll ever see you again."

The teddy bear on the shelf growled softly.

"Bye, Teddy," Tam whispered. "Keep an eye on Blue. And don't talk too much."

He paused outside Mum and Dad's room. Dad was snoring, Mum was whistling gently in her sleep.

"Bye," he whispered. "I'll try and bring Great-grandpa home."

Then he rushed downstairs to the kitchen, picked up his green school rucksack and opened the fridge door. There was his lunch box, all neatly packed for tomorrow. He pushed it into his rucksack, and then at the last minute snatched his dad's and shoved that in too.

"Sorry, Dad, but I'm not allowed to eat any of the food in Faery," he whispered. "Anyway, all they eat is roses and buttercups."

"Now!" said Pix, dancing round with impatience. "Hold my hand."

"Do I have to?" Tam protested.

And before he could think, he felt his tummy turning circles inside him. Lights streamed and rushed and flashed. He was spinning, faster and faster, in a wind that was sparkling like crystals and diamonds. He could feel air swirling round him. He clung onto Pix's hand and laughed with joy.

If Mum and Dad had looked out of
their window they'd have seen what
appeared to be a brilliant blue star
streaking across the sky, trailing a white
spinning twist of air like a comet.
They'd have heard a voice singing out,
"I'm flying, Pix! I'm really flying!" and
another voice shouting, "Hold on
tight!"

But they didn't see, and they didn't
hear, because they were fast asleep.

Faery Again

"Tamlin's back! Prince Tamlin's back!"

Tam opened his eyes to find that he was surrounded by sandy children, all clustering round him, shouting excitedly.

"I did it! I did it all on my own!" Pix skipped a full circle, waving her arms in the air.

Tam gazed over the heads of the fairy children. He recognized some of them. Purple-eyed Elfa laughed at him and held her fist up to her eye as if she was looking through a starburster.

"Am I really here? Am I really back in Faery?" The gorgeous colours and scents around him were so familiar that he felt as if he had never been away. "But we didn't come through the green passage! We didn't see the guardian."

"I was only a baby last time, remember," Pix said. "I didn't have wings."

She had tucked her wings across her back, but every time she turned, they flashed with the brilliant colours of dragonflies. She danced round again, so pleased with herself that she nearly bumped into a tall golden-haired woman, who came running across the grass towards them.

"Well done, Pix!" the woman said.
"The king will be very pleased with
you. Welcome back, Prince Tamlin!"

"You're Tanta, aren't you? I
remember you!" Tam said. "You turned
into a salmon when Elfa threw my
starburster into the pool, and then you
turned into a horse and took me over
the mountains."

"I can't do that again," Tanta said
sadly. "I used up all my power doing
that. But never mind, it was worth it.
This time you'll have to make your
own way to the king, and you'll have
to be quick, and very, very brave. And I
warn you, he's really angry."

Pix stopped dancing. "Why?"

"Not with you, Pix. He's angry with
the fairies who brought the other little
boy."

"She means your great-grandpa," Pix
told Tam. "Toby."

"Toby? Tobit, his fairy name will be.

Well, I'm sorry about what happened if you know him, Prince Tamlin. The fairies who did it have been turned into nightmares, of course – and don't you even think about chopping off their heads like you did last time. They deserve to be nightmares till the next blue moon."

"But why? What have they done?"

"I'm afraid something awful has happened. They've lost him."

"Lost him? Where? How?"

"I don't know," said Tanta. "That's the truth."

When she said that, a little green elf came running towards them, stumbling over his own feet in his great hurry.

"Morva see-saw!" he shouted.

"You saw what happened, Morva?" Tanta asked.

Tam recognized the little elf who had shown him the way to the king's secret tower when he was looking for Blue.

"Tobit snitch-snatched," Morva said. His eyes were bulging out of his head with excitement and fear. "Hag-dam flittered Tobit."

"Ah," said Tanta, "so that was it."

A *wheesssh* of silence fell across the fairy children. Some of them hid their faces in their hands. Morva crept up to Tam and stroked him sadly.

"What did he say?" Tam demanded.

"The Damson-hag has flown away with Tobit," said Tanta. "We'll never find him now."

Pix sank down onto the grass and hugged her knees. "Poor Tobit," she muttered. "Poor, poor Tobit."

"Please tell me who the Damson-hag is, and where she lives, and what she's going to do with my great-grandpa," Tam said.

Tanta shook her head. "I can't tell you anything. I can't speak anything about the Damson-hag. It's forbidden. It's too dangerous for me, or for any of my children here."

"But what can I do?" wailed Tam. "He's my only great-grandpa. Mum says he's an awful nuisance sometimes, and Dad wishes he would go away. He's ever so noisy. But I love him."

Morva tugged at Tanta's skirt. "Flame-reader," he whispered.

"Yes, Flame-reader!" Pix said. She jumped up and danced round Tanta again. "Flame-reader knows everything, doesn't he? We could ask him. I've never even seen him. I've always wanted to see him, Tanta. Can I go? Can I take Tam there?"

"You could try. It won't be easy." Tanta bent down and put both her hands on Tam's shoulders. "You must be very brave, Prince Tamlin. The Flame-reader is the oldest of all the fairies. He knows everything, as Pix said. But he keeps himself away from all of us."

"Morva show path," the elf said. His eyes had grown huge with fright.

"Good." Tanta nodded. "Pix and Morva will show you the way to his cave. It's through the forest of ten thousand soldier trees, that's all I know. But he hates mortals. You must wear your cloak."

Trembling, Tam opened up his

rucksack and pulled out his red dressing gown. As he shook it out it turned into a long velvet cloak.

"And you must use your sword."

"It's only plastic," Tam said, but as he drew it out of his belt it flashed silver. "Vinand'r!" he said proudly. He felt like a real prince now.

"Nightmares will follow you, but remember to leave them behind. The king of the fairies will deal with them, not you! You must not touch them with your sword. And you must be brave. And when you meet the Flame-reader, you must not ask him any questions. Go now, quickly." And unexpectedly Tanta bent down and kissed him. It felt as soft as a butterfly touching his cheek, but it seemed to fill Tam with courage.

"I'm ready." He clutched his sword and looked round. "Come on Morva, come on Pix," he said. "Let's go."

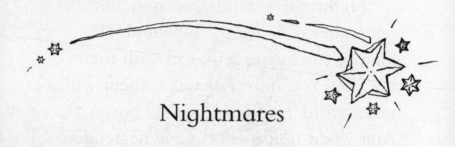

Nightmares

Morva and Pix were so scared that they
held hands as they ran behind Tam.
Morva shouted out directions but he
wouldn't go in front, not for anything.
Far away they could hear terrifying
baying and howling, and before long
wild dogs came pounding towards
them. They had huge heads and yellow
teeth, blazing orange eyes and long
lollopy, dripping tongues. Tam knew
these were the nightmares.

They swirled around Tam and Morva
and Pix, yapping and snarling, growling
and grizzling. Poor little Morva fell
over and lay with his legs kicking the
air, and refused to go any further.

"Morva only elf," he sobbed. "Teeny
tiny elf."

"All right," Tamlin said. "I won't
make you come with me."

The little elf scuttled away like a
rabbit. Pix jumped onto Tam's back and
clung to him, trembling. "Elves are such
cowards, aren't they, Tam?"

"I don't feel very brave myself," Tam said, gripping his sword. He kicked one of the dogs away, and it snapped its yellow fangs at him, drooling slimy green saliva.

"I don't like them," Pix yelled. "Use Vinand'r. Chop off their heads!"

"I want to," Tam said. "I could do that easily, and they'd turn back into fairies and everything would be all right. But Tanta said I mustn't, didn't she? It would make the king angry. Hang on tight, Pix. I'm going to run through them. I've got to, or I'll never find out where Great-grandpa is."

He could see the forest ahead of him, not far now. He closed his eyes and ran as fast as he could, ignoring the nightmares as they leaped and howled around him. He tried to keep his mind fixed on Great-grandpa Toby. And as soon as they reached the edge of the forest of ten thousand soldier trees, something strange happened. The nightmares stopped following him.

They crouched down to the ground with their ears flattened against their heads, and they started whining pitifully. One by one they began to slink away. It seemed that even they were frightened of the Flame-reader, the oldest fairy of them all.

The Forest of Ten Thousand Soldier Trees

Tam lowered Pix down and gazed helplessly at the tangled web of trees and branches and brambles in front of them. He tried to push his way forward, but the branches closed down, barring his way. Twigs snagged his hair, tree roots poked out of the ground like scabby hands, snatching at his feet.

"Is this the only way to the Flame-reader's cave?" he asked.

Pix nodded miserably. "Nobody ever goes in or out," she said.

"I'm not surprised," said Tam. "Those soldier trees will tear us to bits if we ever try to go in there." He sat down on a lumpy tree stump, nearly crying in despair. "We've been so brave. We ran all the way through that pack of nightmare dogs, and we didn't turn back. But this is hopeless. Now we'll never find Great-grandpa Toby."

"Don't break," Pix said. "You're a prince, remember."

Tam stared at her. "Prince Tamlin! Of course I am! I know how we can get through! I can use my sword!" He pulled Vinand'r out of his belt and held it high, so it flashed in the sunlight.

Then he waved it in front of him and hacked his way through the forest, slashing from left to right, round his head, round his feet, and Pix skipped behind him screaming out with delight:

"Take that, you trippy old tree! Take that, you bristly old bramble! You won't stop Prince Tamlin!"

At last they came to a massive shoulder of rock, as black as ebony. A huge hole like a yawning mouth opened up.

They had reached the cave of the Flame-reader.

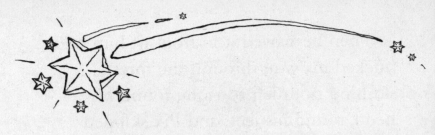

The Flame-Reader

The Flame-reader was standing in front of the cave mouth. At first Tam thought he was an ancient, bent tree. His skin was wrinkled and gnarled and grey like old wood, and his fingers and toes were like twisted twigs. His hair and beard rustled and crackled like clumps of old dry leaves. His eyes were deep, black holes, with no light in them at all.

"Who's making all that noise?" He spoke in a dry, splintery voice.

Tam took a deep breath. "I'm Tam," he said.

"Prince Tamlin," whispered Pix. She was hiding behind him. Tam could feel her trembling. He could hear her teeth chattering.

"I see by your cloak that you are
truly a prince," the crackly voice said. "I
see by your sword that you have
hacked my soldiers down."

"And are you . . . ?" Tam began, but
Pix poked him quickly.

"No questions!" she hissed.

"I mean, you are the Flame-reader."

"I am." The ancient fairy nodded, and his bones creaked, his leafy hair rustled. "What do you want?"

"Where's— Erm, no, I don't mean that. I mean, I want to know where my great-grandpa Toby is. He's very old, you see, and he shouldn't be here at all."

The Flame-reader stood still. For a long time nothing at all happened. "There are no very old mortals in Faery," the splintery voice said at last. "They simply do not come here." He turned, creaking, and began to make his way into the cave.

Pix peered out from behind Tam's back. "Please, oldest of all fairies, I turned him into a little boy.

He's called Tobit here." She dodged back behind Tam, covering her eyes with her fists.

The Flame-reader creaked back round. There was a tiny glimmer in the black holes of his eyes. "Tobit. You want to know where Tobit is?"

"Yes, yes please," stammered Tam.

"You want me to read flames? You want a fire?" The voice crinkled away to nothing.

"I – yes, I think so."

To Tam's horror the Flame-reader began pulling bits off himself and piling them onto the floor of the cave. He held out his right arm to Tam.

"Chop!" he said. "Chop!"

"I can't chop your arm off!" Tam gasped.

"Chop!" the Flame-reader ordered.

"Do it, Tam," Pix whispered.

So Tam raised his sword with both hands and it whistled sharply down

onto the Flame-reader's arm. Snap! The
arm clattered onto the floor of the cave
and broke into twigs. Tam dared himself
to look at the Flame-reader. Little green
buds were growing in his shoulder,
where the arm had been. And where he
had pulled bits off himself, tiny sprigs of
leaves were unfurling.

The Flame-reader leaned towards the
pile of twigs on the cave floor and
rubbed the twiggy fingers of his left
hand together. Smoke and then flames

curled out from the ends of his fingers.
He dropped his hand into the middle of
the stick pile and a slow, greedy fire
began to burn. But where his hand had
been, little green buds were sprouting
from his wrist.

"Fairy magic," Pix murmured.
"That's very clever."

"I thought he was going to die," Tam
whispered back.

"Fairies never die," the Flame-reader
said. His voice was sharper than before,
not nearly so old and splintery. "Watch
the flames, mortal boy. Watch, and
listen, but do not ask."

The flames were licking over the pile of wood. They flickered like coloured flies, from one colour to another, emerald and ruby, peacock, silver, peach, sunshine, every colour you would ever imagine, and they twisted and writhed into endless shapes and patterns. At last all the colours seemed to mingle together and become a hazy blue, and then just a few white wisps, and the fire died.

"What did you see?" the Flame-reader asked.

"Colours and lights," Tam said. "It was very beautiful. But what – where . . . ?" No, he mustn't ask questions, he remembered. "Oldest of all fairies, you read the flames. You know where Tobit is."

"Tobit is trapped in a golden cage. The Damson-hag has the key, and will never part with it."

Tam bit his lips and waited. He was

bursting to ask who, and why, and where, and how, but he knew he mustn't. The Flame-reader would tell him everything he wanted to know, or he would tell him nothing at all. Tam waited and waited, and at last the Flame-reader began to speak.

"Why should I tell you anything else?" he roared, his voice full and strong and young again. He pointed a bent finger at Pix, who was shivering with fright. "I have a mind to turn you into a nightmare for your part in this! Better still, as you seem to love going to mortal-land so much, I think I will make you stay there. I will turn you into a slug, and you will sit inside a daffodil trumpet for ever. Men will squeeze you and poison you and drown you, thrushes will eat you, but you will never die because you are a disgraced fairy. Every year you will be back again, another slug in another daffodil."

"But oldest of fairies, I only did what the king asked me to do," Pix pleaded.

The Flame-reader ignored her. He turned to Tam. "And as for you, I will turn you into a soldier tree. Your bones will turn to wood, your blood will turn to sap, your toes will root you to the ground."

Tam looked with horror at his feet to see if it was happening yet. He wriggled his toes fiercely. But when he looked up, he saw that the Flame-reader was laughing.

"I could do these things, but I won't.

You may not be a real prince, but you are as brave as anyone I have ever met. I have decided to help you instead. I will tell you the story of the Damson-hag."

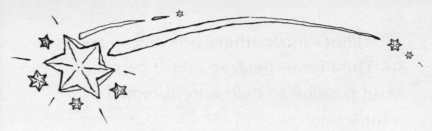

The Flame-Reader's Story

"I haven't seen the Damson-hag for thousands of years," he began. "She was once very beautiful. She has a son who is also beautiful. He is the king of the fairies."

Tam swallowed hard. So many questions were bubbling up now that he felt as if he was eating them to keep them from bursting out.

"The fairy king loves man-magic. He wanted a tube that is so magical that when you look through it the world breaks up into little pieces."

"That's my starburster!" Tam gasped.

The Flame-reader nodded. "Exactly. And now he has it, he wants a stick that sings."

"Great-grandpa's humming machine."

"And he can't have it!" the Flame-reader roared again. "We want no more of this meddling with mortals. We have our own magic here. Man-magic could destroy us. We have no need of it!"

Tam thought about all the things that were different about Faery. He thought about the colours and the brightness, the scents and sounds, everything so much clearer than anything he had ever known before. And then he thought about home – the buildings everywhere, cars and planes, litter, crowds, computers, television, mobile phones. Nothing was the same.

He thought about missiles and war, things he had seen on the television news. Was that what the Flame-reader meant? Could he see all these things when he looked into the flames?

"I know," he whispered. "It's lovely here. It's like a lovely dream."

The Flame-reader nodded. "So leave it to us." His voice was gentle now. "We don't want anything to do with mortals here. Find the boy Tobit, and take him home. The Damson-hag wants to keep him because of the magic he has brought with him. Take him away from her, and keep him away from the king of the fairies. Will you do that? Never let him come here again. Do you hear me? Do you promise?"

"Yes," said Tam, shaking again. "I promise."

"Now I will tell you where to find him. Follow the white path. Look neither over your left shoulder nor over your right shoulder. Never turn back, whatever you may hear. But when the ruby cockerel crows, look for the golden feather and keep it safe. Then follow the stinking fox. I give you Spinner to help you in your task."

He held up his hand, and a silver spider bobbed down like a yo-yo from his finger.

The Flame-reader wrapped her thread round Tam's wrist, then gave a deep sigh like the sound of wind in fir trees, and simply disappeared. His cave disappeared, and the tangled forest that surrounded it. The day disappeared and turned into hollow night. Deep, velvet blackness was all around, except for a streak of moonlight on the ground.

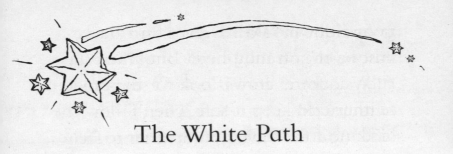

The White Path

"That was freaky!" Tam moved his hand up and down, and Spinner bobbed with him, then seemed to eat up the silver thread she had made, until she was tucked under his wrist.

"I've always wanted my very own spider," Tam said happily.

"The Flame-reader is so clever!" sighed Pix. "I can't wait till I can do that sort of magic. It takes about ten thousand years to be able to disappear."

"It's all very well for him, just going off like that, leaving us in the dark. I don't like it. What are we supposed to do now?"

"Follow the white path!" Pix jumped

up and down. "Didn't you listen? It must be this streak of moonlight."

"Well, for a start, it doesn't seem to go anywhere, just a few paces," Tam said. "And for a next, I'm starving. I'm not going anywhere till I've had a sandwich."

He sat down on the moonlight strip and took his lunch box out of his rucksack. "Do you want cheese and tomato or egg and cress?"

"I can't eat your disgusting food," Pix said. "Haven't you got any nice rosebuds in there?"

"The Flame-reader was right, you'd make a really good slug." Tam giggled.

"You'll have to make do with a bit of cress." He pulled some green stuff like strands of hair out of his sandwich and passed them to Pix. Spinner sang to herself in a high, sweet voice. "Sorry I haven't got any bluebottles for you," Tam told her. "Do you want some breadcrumbs?"

At last Tam was ready to go on. Pix insisted on having a piggyback again, as she was too tired to walk or fly. She perched on his rucksack and said she didn't mind about the lunch boxes at all, they made a nice seat. A moment later, she was fast asleep.

Tam stood in the middle of the moonlit patch and took a step forward, and then another. The path opened up in front of him as if a white carpet was being rolled away, a bit at a time, from under his feet. He walked on steadily, careful not to let his feet stray off into the darkness at either side. At first he

could hear nothing except the sound of
his footsteps, and sometimes a contented
snore from Pix. Spinner's tiny spidery
song spiralled around him, high and
sweet and very comforting.

Suddenly there was a shout behind
him. Tam stopped and listened. There it
came again. "Prince Tamlin! Prince
Tamlin!"

Pix was wide awake now. "Don't look round," she hissed.

But the shout came again. It sounded like the Flame-reader's voice.

"Turn, turn, that way spells danger. You've gone the wrong way. Come back. *Come back.*"

"It's not him," Pix whispered.

"It *is* him! It's his voice."

"But you mustn't look back. He said so. Remember?"

"I know," said Tam. "*Look neither over your left shoulder nor over your right shoulder,* he said. But what if he's trying to tell me I've gone the wrong way?"

"But there isn't another white path. Go on, Tam."

Tam took another step forward.

"Danger!" the voice called. "Turn back."

Tam stopped, worried.

The night was full of noise now, all kinds of noises – animal shrieks and howls, wild laughter, whisperings and moanings. The white path shrivelled under his feet and disappeared. Only darkness lay ahead.

"This way, this way," whispered the voice, smooth as a cat. It was just behind his left shoulder. "Turn this way, and you'll be safe."

"No, no, I won't go that way," Tam said firmly.

The sound came at his right side, shrieking now, wailing and angry, ten voices or more, like a yard of fighting cats.

"This way, this way."

He put his hands over his ears and shut his eyes tight. He felt himself being spun round like a leaf in the wind. Spinner crawled into his palm and tucked herself inside it, trembling. Pix put her arms round his neck and clung on, gasping for breath. At last the spinning stopped. Tam was so dizzy he could hardly stand upright. He opened his eyes slowly and waited for the world to be still again.

"Go forward, Prince Tamlin," Pix urged.

But ahead of him was complete blackness. He had no idea which way he was facing. What if the path lay in the other direction now? The voice was still swirling around him like a zizzing insect now, an annoying bluebottle. He lifted his hand as if to swish it away, and at the same time he lifted his foot to step forward. Two things happened. Spinner shot out from under his palm and strangled the insect voice as if she were eating a fly. Zzzzzgulp! It was gone. And the white path ribboned out again ahead of Tam.

He ran along the path. Whatever it was that the Flame-reader had sent to test him had been beaten and eaten. Surely nothing could go wrong.

"What else did the Flame-reader tell us, Pix?" he asked, but she was fast asleep again already.

Spinner sang softly to herself: "*Never turn back. When the ruby cockerel crows, look for the golden feather. Keep it safe. Follow the stinking fox.*" The song made a chiming beat for Tam to run to.

The darkness around them began to fade to a pearly grey. Dawn was coming. A ruby-red cockerel strutted onto the path ahead of Tam.

"*Cock-a-doodle-doo!*" It held up its crimson-crest head and crowed loudly, then clattered away again, dropping a feather as it flew. It shone like a golden arrow.

"*Pick it up! Pick it up and keep it safe!*" Tam laughed. "I remember!" He picked the feather up and stuck it in his hair. Instantly the air was filled with sunlight, and the white moon path disappeared. Little paths ran in every direction, like the tracks rabbits make in the grass.

Tam stood with his hands on his hips, gazing in despair at the maze of trails. "Now which way?"

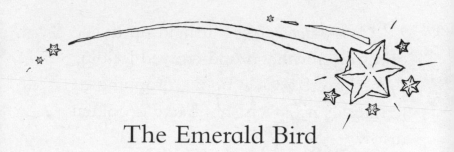

The Emerald Bird

Pix yawned sleepily, and Tam set her down on the ground.

"Which way?" she asked, rubbing her eyes. She looked up at Tam. "Oh, I like your feather."

Spinner bobbed up and down on her thread, twisting this way and that like the needle of a compass. "Which way, which way?"

Something unseen rustled in front of them, then a snake slid onto one of the tracks. It was green and gold, just the colour of sunlight on grass. It turned its head towards them.

"Thissss way," it hissed. "Ssssee me come, ssssee me go." It coiled away and was lost in the grass.

"Did the Flame-reader tell us to
follow a snake?" Tam asked.

"Yessss," came a hiss, and now they
could see it again, twisting and coiling
through the yellow and green of the
grass.

"Wait for us!" Tam shouted.

He and Pix started after it.

"No!" squealed Spinner. "Don't go that way! It's leading you astray!" and at that moment the snake twisted

towards them, its eyes as bright as jewels in its head. Its tongue streaked out and snatched Spinner from Tam's wrist.

"Oh no!" Pix shouted. "It's eaten Spinner!"

But Tam was just as quick as the snake had been. He pulled his sword out of his belt. "Vinand'r!" he shouted, and with one swipe he chopped off the snake's head.

Spinner scuttled out of the snake's mouth and up the sword, and hid herself in Tam's sleeve. The snake grew another head, but it was the head of a mouse, with a pointed nose and shivery whiskers.

"I did that!" Pix said, dancing with excitement. "Tam, I did that trick! A snake with a mouse's head! Whee!"

The snake squeaked and twisted away quickly.

"Whee! Whee! Follow me!" a high birdsong voice twittered. Now a bird with wings the colour of emeralds flashed around them. Tam could feel his hair lifting with the wind it made as it fluttered round his head. It soared away from them. "Follow me!"

"How can we follow a bird?" he asked. "It's flying too fast!"

Way up in the sky, the emerald bird dipped and flashed its wings.

Pix unfurled her own wings and fluttered them prettily. "I can do that. Hold my hand, Tam."

"But it's flying so high." Tam shielded his eyes and peered up at the bird. "Wait a minute!" he shouted. "It's stolen my feather!"

Sure enough, they could see something golden and shiny in the bird's beak.

"I'll get it back!" Pix said. She spread out her wings and soared up like the bird, over Tam's head, higher and higher, swooping and circling and laughing out loud just for the fun of it. Tam shielded his eyes with his hand and watched helplessly. He saw Pix closing in on the emerald bird, faster and faster. Then the bird turned and flapped its wings at Pix. They seemed to be fighting in mid-air, tossing this way and that way like coloured rags on a washing line.

"Pix, Pix, be careful!" Tam called.

One of them broke away from the other. Because the sun was so bright behind them it was impossible for Tam to see which one was which, bird or Pix. One flew away, and one fell, spinning at first, and then dropping like a stone out of the sky.

It was Pix.

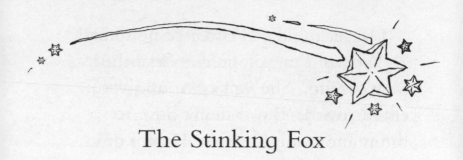

The Stinking Fox

"Pix, oh Pix!" Tam ran to where she lay stretched out on the ground. "Pix, are you all right?"

To his great relief Pix sat up and shook her wings crossly. They looked very untidy now, a bit tattered and covered with dust. "Stupid floppy old bird," she muttered.

"Never mind the bird. Are you hurt?"

"Course I'm not. Fairies never hurt. Stop fussing." She was obviously very embarrassed. "But it didn't have to throw me away like that. Here. Look after it this time."

She held out the golden feather.

"Pix, you're perfect!" Tam told her. He tucked the feather into his belt, next to Vinand'r. "I was just worried. I don't know what I'd do without you. You're my best friend."

"Am I, Tam?" She beamed happily at him and folded her wings away. "That's all right then. Now, what were we doing?"

"We were trying to find the way," Tam reminded her. "We shouldn't have followed the snake or the bird. Oh, I wish I could remember what the Flame-reader told us next. Follow the white path. We did that. Look neither over the right shoulder nor over the left shoulder. Did that. Found the golden feather. But then? Oh, wait a minute—!" He stepped forward and sniffed, then held his nose. "There's something very smelly round here." He was aware of a strong, sharp smell. "Fox!" he shouted. "That was the next thing. Follow the stinking fox!"

And now they could see it, streaking ahead of them like a tongue of flame, an orange flicker in the long grass. They ran after it, darting backwards and forwards just as the fox was doing. Once it crouched down and turned its head towards them, panting.

"We're not hunting you, mister smelly fox," Tam shouted. "We're following you."

The fox opened his mouth and laughed, and set off again.

And then, very faint, very far away, came the sound of music. It was soft and sad and low. The more they followed the stinking fox, the louder it grew. It was a buzzy sort of music, a bees-in-a-jar-of-honey sort of music. There was no mistaking the sound.

"That's Great-grandpa Toby's humming machine," said Tam. "We've found him!"

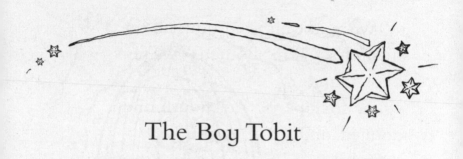

The Boy Tobit

Now they could see a large golden cage dangling from a tree. It was rocking gently backwards and forwards, pushed by a sleepy old midnight-blue bear. Inside the cage sat a boy of about nine. His head was bowed down and his legs were crossed. He was playing a harmonica. The tune he was playing was so sad that it was almost like crying.

"It's him, it's Tobit!" squealed Pix excitedly. "I did it! I did it! I found him, all by myself!"

"No, you didn't," said Tam. "And anyway, that's not Great-grandpa Toby. That's just a boy."

The boy in the cage stopped playing
and looked up. "My word!" he said. "It's
Tam! How did you get here?"

Tam couldn't stop staring at the boy.
It was just as if he was looking at
himself in a mirror — the same untidy
hair, the same brown eyes. He suddenly
realized that the boy in the cage *was*
Great-grandpa Toby, just as he must
have looked when he was only nine
years old. He went right up to the cage

and shook the bars. The door was firmly locked.

"I'll get you out," he promised. "Oh, poor Great-grandpa!" He turned to Pix. "This is all your fault. Can't you do something to help him?"

He heard the sound of cackly laughter, and turned to see a woman coming towards them. She was very bent and ugly, with long, straggly, tangled seaweed hair and dark purple rings round her eyes. From her red sash hung a key, surely the key to the cage.

"Another mortal child!" she said in her crackly voice. "How lucky I am! And you have a fairy child with you." She scratched Pix's chin with her crooked nails. "Do you really expect *her* to break my enchantment? Mine, the queen of all queens?" and then she cooed sweetly. "Tobit is my own darling, my little hummingbird. Aren't you, my sweet?" she purred. "Sing for me, my precious."

Great-grandpa Toby put the harmonica to his mouth and played a lovely lilting tune, and the Damson-hag hobbled about in a stooped, stiff-legged dance. But as she danced something strange happened to her. Her movements became light and graceful, willowy as a young girl's. Her face grew young, her eyes shone, and were the rich colour of plums. Her matted hair became smooth and shining, swaying around her like a beautiful shimmering purple cloak.

"Mine, mine, mine," she sang. "You're my own darling hummingbird."

Tam couldn't take his eyes off her. He had never seen anyone more beautiful, or more frightening. As she danced, her shadow danced with her, a deep purple-red. It was as if there were two of her, swaying and dancing around him, laughing, while the harmonica played on.

"Dance with me, boy, dance with me!" She took hold of Tam's hands. Her fingers were icy cold. He found that he couldn't stand still. His feet were moving in time to the music. The midnight-blue bear stood up on his hind legs and rocked the cage, his huge paws padding up and down gracefully. He rumbled the tune in a deep growly voice.

"That's it, my bear pet, sing for me." The Damson-hag laughed.

And underneath the sound of her laughter and the bear's deep rumbling growl came another sound, breathy and wheezy and hardly heard, a strange, tinny song to the dancing tune:

"With golden needle and silver thread
Capture a queen in a silken web . . ."

someone seemed to be singing, very softly. It was almost as if the words were coming from the humming machine itself. It was obvious that the Damson-hag hadn't heard it. She swung Tam round and then, suddenly bored, let go of his hands. She snapped her fingers and stopped dancing. The music stopped instantly.

"Don't think you can take my hummingbird away from me," she snapped at Tam. "He's mine for ever."

She tipped the cage with her fingers so it began to rock again. "Carry on, bear," she hissed sharply. "Do your job. Or we'll get this nice boy to do it for you. I'm sure he'd like to stay here too."

She waltzed away, laughing, and as she entered the darkness of the trees her voice grew old and cracked again, her figure stooped, her hair straggly and wild. "In fact," she cackled, "he won't be leaving for a long, long time. He's mine now. Mine! You're all mine! Every one of you!"

"You're All Mine!"

"My word," said Great-grandpa Toby.
"It's very cramped in this cage. I could
do with stretching my legs a bit."

Tam tried the door again. "It's no
good, I can't open it."

Pix pulled at his arm. "Come away,
Price Tamlin. You heard what she said.
Get away while we have the chance."

"Not without my great-grandpa,"
said Tam firmly.

"But how can we take him? She's got
the key."

"I know." Tam nodded, frowning. "I
saw it when she was dancing."

"She's very good at dancing, isn't
she?" Great-grandpa sighed. "She's so
kind, and so beautiful."

"She is beautiful, isn't she?" Tam agreed. "But she's so ugly too! I don't know how she does that."

"My music does it," said Great-grandpa proudly. "My music makes her as beautiful as she was when she was young. That's why I'm here, she says. I'm so happy."

Tam gasped with surprise. "Don't you *mind* being here?"

"Well, I'm a bit stiff, and I'm very hungry, but apart from that, no. I'm very lucky, having her to look at all day. She always looks beautiful to me now."

"She's enchanted him," said Pix. "Very clever, I must say."

"Starving hungry," Great-grandpa went on. "I've just about had enough of those petals she keeps giving me. Not enough for a spider to eat, they aren't. Oh, you've got one, I see."

Spinner bobbed down from Tam's

wrist and scuttled up and down the
bars of the cage.

"That's how she's done it, giving you
fairy food," Pix told him. "Don't you
eat any more of those flowers – and
don't you touch them either, Prince
Tamlin. Save them for me. She's nearly
enchanted you already, making you
dance with her like that."

"But she is very beautiful," Tam
sighed.

"There! I knew it," Pix said. "You're
going to have to be very careful, or
she'll be putting you in a cage next."

"Was that thunder, or was it my tummy rumbling?" Great-grandpa asked.

"Just a minute. At least I can give you something to eat." Tam opened up his rucksack and took out his dad's lunch box. "I brought something for you. I think it's Stilton cheese and onion sandwiches. Very smelly anyway. What a pong! Just like your socks, Great-grandpa – I mean, when you *were* a great-grandpa."

"Just the job!" Great-grandpa Toby stretched his hands out between the bars of the cage and munched cheerfully.

"You might *feel* happy here," Tam said. "But you didn't *sound* happy when we arrived. You were playing such a sad tune."

"Oh, the humming machine just seems to play what it wants to play." It was hard to hear what he was saying with his mouth full.

Tam stared at him. "You mean, when you were playing just now, it was really the humming machine making the music?"

Great-grandpa nodded happily. "I just suck and blow, suck and blow, and out comes the music. My word, I bet you thought I was a wonderful player!"

"But what about the song? It was singing words. Real words – and it wasn't you doing it?"

Great-grandpa shook his head.

"It was telling us something!" Pix said. "Remember what it said, Tam?"

Tam frowned. "Something golden,

something silver . . ." He sighed. "No. I can't remember. See if it will sing again."

Great-grandpa picked up the harmonica and blew and sucked. Not a sound came out of it. "Hope I haven't got crumbs in it," he said anxiously.

"Something about capturing a queen . . ." muttered Pix. They stared at each other. "Try to remember, Tam."

The midnight bear stopped rocking the cage and rumbled to himself. Spinner stood with two of her arms folded.

*"With golden needle
and silver thread
Capture a queen in a
silken web . . ."*

she sang in her tiny,
high-pitched voice.

"My word!" said Great-grandpa.
"What a clever spider."

But Pix was leaping around in great
excitement. "I did it! I did it! I did it all
on my—"

"Shush," said Tam. "We haven't done
it yet."

They could see the Damson-hag
coming back towards them, stooping
stiffly every now and again to pick
flowers.

"Quick! She's coming," Tam said. "A
golden needle — where can I get one?"

"How is my precious hummingbird?"
the Damson-hag croaked. "I've brought
you a feast, my darling. Rose petals,

pink and white and red. And some for
your dear little friend. My pretty little
dancing boy."

"A needle, a needle," Tam whispered.
"Quick, someone, or she'll trap us all."

Pix jumped up and plucked the
cockerel feather out of Tam's belt.

"There!" she said triumphantly.

"Pix, you're fantastic!" Tam knelt
down and put the feather on the
ground. With the point
of his sword he
carefully pierced a hole
in the stem of the
feather. He held it up.
"A golden needle!" he
said triumphantly.

The bear growled.

"And a lily full of nectar for you all
to drink," the Damson-hag purred. She
had almost reached the cage.

"Silver thread?" Tam whispered.
"Quick!"

Spinner yodelled and swung down.
Her thread spiralled behind her. Pix
threaded one end through the hole in
the feather. Spinner dangled upside
down, spinning more thread as fast as
she could.

"Quick, oh quick, oh quick!" said
Pix. "Give me the needle, Tam."

"Little games?" laughed the Damson-
hag sweetly. Then she kicked out
viciously at Pix. "Out of my way, fairy
flea."

At first she couldn't understand what
Pix was doing, or why she was jumping
around her so excitedly, running
backwards and forwards with a feather
in her hand and a spider bobbing
behind her. She tried to kick her away
again, then realized that her legs
wouldn't move. She was bound tight,
tight, in the web that Pix was sewing
round her.

"Let me go!" she roared.

Her ankles were sewn together, then
her fingers, then her hands. It was the
magic sent by the Flame-reader, and it
was stronger than anything she could
do. It was powerful and completely
unbreakable.

"Get me out of here! Let me go!" she screamed. "I'll turn you into scratchy cats! I'll turn your bones to jelly! I'll make you hop like frogs! I'll give you fishy fins! I'll – I'll – I'll—"

Tam ran towards her and pulled at the key that dangled from her red sash. With one strike of his sword he  slashed the sash and the key fell into his hand.

He dashed to the cage and unlocked the door, and Great-grandpa tumbled out.

"Come on!" Tam shouted. "Leave her like that! She can't harm us now."

"I'll plague you with ants, I'll blister your feet, I'll . . ." and then there was nothing more the Damson-hag could say, because Pix sewed up her mouth.

They were free.

The Midnight Bear

They had no idea which way to run.
Pix wasn't very good at running
because her legs were so short. She
opened her wings and fluttered them so
her feet lifted off the ground every now
and again. But no matter how fast they
ran or flew, they could hear the sound
of heavy feet lumbering after them. Pix
glanced over her shoulder.

"It's the midnight bear," she panted.
"We'll have to run very fast to get away
from him. I could fly one of you, if you
hold my hand. But I can't fly two."

Great-grandpa Toby tripped and fell
over. "Go on without me," he panted.

"No way!" Tam said. "He won't

harm us, Great-grandpa. I won't let
him." He drew out his sword and flashed
it above his head. "Vinand'r!" he shouted.

"My word!" Great-grandpa said.
"You couldn't really kill a bear, could
you?"

"Of course he could!" said Pix. "At it,
Sir Tamlin! Swipe his head off!"

But Tam knew he wouldn't do it. His
hands were shaking and his mouth was
as dry as paper. "Go away, Midnight
Bear!" he tried to shout, but his voice
came out as thin as a mouse-squeak,
and the great blue-black bear lumbered
towards them. Then it stopped and
reared up on his great back legs.

"Nix bad bear!" he rumbled, and he
held out his paw towards Tam.
Dangling from it was the golden key.
"For Prince."

"What do I want that for?" Tam
asked, lowering his sword. He took the
key carefully from the bear.

The bear rubbed his paws together,
then he mimed lifting something up,
putting it inside something, closing a
door, and turning a key in a lock.

"Haggy," he chuckled deep in his
throat. "Haggy-house!" He broke out
into loud roars of laughter.

Pix was the only one to understand him. "You've put the Damson-hag in the cage, and locked it?" she asked.

The midnight bear laughed, still chuckling, and beat his chest with his paws in triumph.

Tam put his sword away. "Then you'd better come with us," he said.

So there were five of them: Tam and Great-grandpa, Pix and the midnight bear, and little bobbing Spinner, and they still had no idea where they were going, or why. But the way itself seemed clear enough, because stretching ahead was an avenue of flowers, opening up to them as they walked; every colour you could dream of, and more. The scent was rich and sweet. As they walked, Pix plucked petals and nibbled them, and every now and then the midnight bear stooped and helped himself to a handful.

"Are you really a bear?" Tam asked.

"I'm sure they eat more than that."

"Haggy-wist," he grumbled.

"The Damson-hag enchanted him," Pix translated. "He's really an elf, I think. He speaks Old Faery. Only elves talk it these days."

"Can't you turn him back?"

"Break the Damson-hag's enchantment!" Pix's eyes were wide with fear. "I can't do that! I'm only a childling. *You* must do it."

"How? I don't know any magic."

"You'll find a way, Prince Tamlin."

Tam sighed. "I don't know how to do it. And I don't know how to get Great-grandpa Toby home. I promised the Flame-reader I'd do it. *Find the boy Tobit, and take him home*, he told me."

"Well," Pix murmured uncomfortably, "I don't think that's going to be possible. Can you hear anything, Tam?"

There was a distant sound of

galloping hooves and jingling harnesses, the flapping of banners, shouts and cries, growing steadily closer. Suddenly they were surrounded by prancing horses, black, white, silver, green, deep ocean-blue, and riding them were knights dressed in black velvet. And watching them from one side were two figures that Tam recognized. One was dressed all in white, with white hair like a crown of dandelion fluff. The other had a long gown as blue as the sky, and hair like a drift of white snow.

The king and queen of the fairies.

Fairy Bargains

"At last," said the king, dismounting from his horse. "My childhood friend."

He walked straight up to Great-grandpa Toby and held out both of his hands. "Welcome! Welcome to Faery, young Tobit, prince of mortals. Welcome to the land of King Oban and Queen Tania."

"My word," said Great-grandpa. "My word." He hadn't any more words to say, because he was so amazed, and happy, and frightened, all at the same time.

"And welcome back, Prince Tamlin."

Tam bowed. He glanced nervously at the queen of the fairies, not knowing whether he should bow to her or kiss her hand or what, but the queen seemed far more interested in Great-grandpa Toby. They all did, in fact. The knights were jostling each other to get a better look at him, as if he were a pop star or something. The king was still holding both of Great-grandpa's hands, smiling at him as if he were his long-lost brother.

"We met so long ago, and here we are again after all these years — and you're still a boy and I'm still a king!"

"I'm over ninety really," Great-grandpa chuckled.

"I still have your magic seeing stick," King Oban said, "that Prince Tamlin gave me in exchange for his sister. It is a wonderful thing indeed, but it doesn't work properly." He let go of Great-grandpa at last and produced the kaleidoscope.

"My starburster!" said Tam.

"You look," said the king of the
fairies. "You mend it."

He gave it to Great-grandpa Toby,
who peered through it, twisting it this
way and that, chuckling in amazement.

"My word! I've never seen it behave
like this!"

King Oban stamped his foot. "The
colours are wishy-washy!" he grumbled.
"They're old and broken!"

Great-grandpa took the starburster
away from his eye and gazed around at
the dazzling colours of the flowers
everywhere. He looked through the
starburster again and then took it away
from his eye.

"You're right," he said. "It's because

the colours here are so very, very beautiful and dazzling that they can't get any better. So when you look through the starburster they look paler than they really are, and you see them in little pieces instead of whole and lovely. In my land, it makes the flowers glow like fairy flowers. My word" – he twisted the starburster again and smiled – "it works very differently here. It doesn't do this where I come from."

The king stamped his foot again. "Mend it!" he shouted.

"I can't," Great-grandpa said. "It's not broken, you see. It just works differently here."

"I'll have it back then," said Tam, stretching out his hand for it.

"Oh no," said the king. He took the starburster away from Great-grandpa and folded his arms. "A gift for a gift. I give you the seeing stick if you give me the singing stick."

"The singing stick?" Great-grandpa repeated. "Ah! You mean my humming machine!" He frowned. "But it's my special thing. It makes me happy when I'm sad, and it makes me dream, and it makes people dance. It's my special thing."

"Give it!" the king ordered. Reluctantly Great-grandpa took the little silver box out of his pocket. He opened it and stroked the velvet lining, then took out the harmonica and snapped the box shut.

"Play it," the king said. "Here, Prince."

He tossed the starburster to Tam, who hugged it as if he could never let it go.

He turned away from the king and looked down it, and saw something so wonderful and beautiful that he wanted to cry, something that he never thought he would see again. He could see a garden with a scruffy lawn and pale yellow flowers. He could see an old apple tree. He knew that tree. He knew that garden. He swivelled the starburster round a bit, so he was looking through the window of a house into a room. There was a baby's cot, and in the cot, his own little sister, Baby Blue, smiling as if she could see him.

Then Great-grandpa began to play his humming machine. He played the happy dancing tune that he used to play at home. Tam swivelled the starburster again, and saw Mum coming into the room. She stooped down and lifted Blue out of her cot, and started dancing around the room with her. It was as if she could *hear* the tune.

Tam looked up and saw that
everyone around him was dancing too
– the king and queen, the midnight-
blue bear, Pix, everyone, arms in the air,
faces full of laughter. Even the horses
carrying the knights were shifting their
hooves up and down in time to the
music. Great-grandpa stopped playing
and the king held out his hand.

"Mine now," he said.

Great-grandpa risked a wink at Tam,
and Tam knew then that he had seen
what Tam had seen when he looked
through the starburster. He turned back
to the king.

"Ah no," he said. "A gift for a gift. I
give you my humming machine if you
take the enchantment away from the
midnight bear."

There was a gasp of surprise from
everyone. Pix pulled a face at Great-
grandpa and shook her head. One of
the knights jerked his horse forward and
leaned down to grab the harmonica
out of Great-grandpa Toby's hand. But
the king raised his hand and the knight
trotted his horse back a pace or two.

"Well, Tobit. So you have learned
quickly about fairy bargaining." King
Oban's smile turned to anger. "I didn't
place the enchantment on the bear in
the first place. You want me to meddle
with someone else's magic?"

"I do," said Tam's brave little great-grandpa. His knees were knocking together, but he held the humming machine tightly in his hand behind his back. "If you know how to, that is," he added daringly.

"I know how to!" the king roared. "I need to think, that's all."

He went over to the midnight bear, who started mumbling anxiously to himself. "Lixen bear offright."

"He said he quite likes being a bear really," Pix whispered to Tam. "But I think he's just scared, don't you?"

King Oban stared into the bear's eyes. Then he turned to Great-grandpa. "If I take away the bear's enchantment for *ever*, I will make one last bargain with you. Do you agree?"

"Well, what is it?" Great-grandpa asked nervously.

"Ah, I'll tell you that when I change the bear back. Agree or not? If you don't agree, he turns back into a bear every night."

"All right. I agree."

"First, the humming machine." King Oban held out his hand, and Great-grandpa Tobit tossed the harmonica across to him. The king put it to his mouth and blew a growly, nasty tune on it. He shook it and frowned and tried again. Nothing but tinny ugliness.

"You'll soon pick it up," Tam promised him. "I did. But what about the bear?"

"Oh, the stupid bear," the king snapped moodily. He clicked his tongue three times and started to play the humming machine again. This time the midnight bear started dancing, though it wasn't much of a tune and it wasn't much of a dance, but it was as if he just couldn't help himself. He turned round and round, stamping his feet crazily, and the moment the music stopped he

did a backward somersault and turned
into a green elf.

"Morva!" Tam gasped. "It was you
all the time! How did you get turned
into a bear?"

"Morva haggy-plix-plee savio Tobit,"
the little elf gabbled. "Stead haggy-wist
biggybluey bear."

"My word," said Great-grandpa.
"What was all that about?"

"Ssh!" whispered Pix. "Don't let the
king hear. He said he went to the
Damson-hag to try to rescue Tobit, but
she turned him into a bear instead."

"Well, he was a very brave elf to try,"
Tam whispered.

Morva chuckled with pride.

The king interrupted them. "Now,
Tobit, I have one last bargain to make,
and there will be no more between us.
My gift for your gift for my gift for
your gift is this: I took away the bear's
enchantment. Now you must ride on
my horse."

Great-grandpa's eyes shone. To ride on that beautiful silver-white horse, with its golden mane and tail and its reins all crusted with jewels! Why would the king want him to do that?

"No!" Tam said suddenly. "Don't do it!" and so did Pix, and so did Spinner in her tiny spirally voice, and so did Morva the elf. They all said it at the same time.

But Great-grandpa, silly little nine-year-old boy Great-grandpa Toby said, "Yes! Oh, yes *please!*"

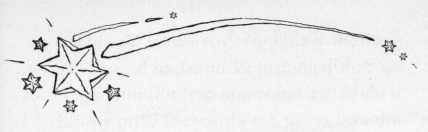

The King of the Fairies

The king signalled to one of the knights
to raise the stirrups of his horse so a
child could ride it.

"Tobit!" he called at last. "We are
ready!"

At first it was hard to understand
what was happening. Great-grandpa
grinned excitedly at Tam and walked
up to the towering silver horse. Then
the king took off his own gleaming
white cloak and flung it round Great-
grandpa's shoulders. The knights
cheered and roared and threw handfuls
of glittering stars into the air, and the
stars bloomed silver trails like fireworks.
Great-grandpa was lifted high, high up

onto the saddle of the horse. The queen
trotted her sky-blue horse up to join his.

And the king went down on his
knees.

At last Tam was able to make out
what everyone was shouting.

"Hail! Hail the new king!"

"Pix? What does it mean?" he asked.

But Pix was dancing up and down, waving her arms and shouting with all the others. "Hail, King Tobit! King of the fairies!" she was shouting.

Tam ran forward, but the knights barred his way with their horses. King Tobit laughed joyfully down at him. He looked as if he would burst with pride.

"Do you hear that, Tam! King of the fairies! That's me!"

"And I am Oban again, at last!" the dandelion-headed king-that-used-to-be sighed, such a deep, deep sigh of pleasure that it was obvious that this was what he had wanted all the time.

The chief knight blew a sapphire horn, and they galloped away, all the black velvet knights, all the blue and scarlet and ruby horses, Pix and Morva and all, away they went, leaving Tam alone.

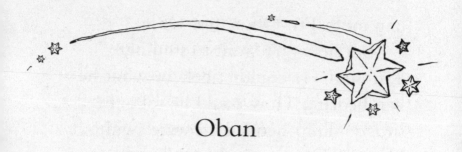

Oban

"Well, Prince Tamlin. There's just us now."

Tam turned to see that the fairy who used to be king was still there, smiling at him.

"It's just a joke, isn't it?" Tam asked. "He'll be coming back soon, won't he? And then I can take him home."

"Not a joke," Oban replied. "He's taken my place. Oh no, he's not going home. But I am."

"What do you mean?"

"I'm coming to the land of mortals." The fairy clapped his hands with joy. "I'm coming home with you! It's what I've always wanted. I'm not the king any more. I'm Oban. Just Oban."

"But he won't want to stay here,"
Tam said. He couldn't believe what he
was hearing. How could he take this
strange fluffy-headed creature (without
his magnificent robe he looked more
like a dandelion than ever) home with
him? What would Mum and Dad say?

"You'll hate our food," he muttered.

"Puff! I can eat your garden," Oban
said. "Pix told me you have roses and
all sorts of flowers there."

"Not in winter. And Mum won't like it if you eat her roses. And anyway, what's Great—"

"King Tobit."

"All right, King Tobit, what's he going to eat?"

"Is that all you think about? Food?"

"Mostly," Tam admitted. His tummy was rumbling even as he spoke.

"Then stop being selfish," Oban said. "A fairy eats fairy food. Your great-grandpa has wanted to come here all his life, ever since he stood outside the green passage and knew it led to Faery; ever since he and I met when he was really nine years old. This is the best thing that's ever happened to him. This is what he has always dreamed about. Why take it away from him?"

Tam remembered Great-grandpa's face when he climbed up onto King Oban's horse, with the white robe gleaming round his shoulders. He had looked more excited and happy than anyone Tam had ever seen. And at home he was often sad because he couldn't do this and couldn't do that any more, couldn't climb trees, couldn't play football, couldn't bend to tie his shoelaces. Maybe he wouldn't get any older in Faery. Maybe he wouldn't die.

"Now," said Oban. "I'm ready to go, aren't you?" He puffed and blew on the humming machine, making awful noises. "The green passage is over that glass hill. We'll get there very soon."

Tam realized that all the time he had been thinking, they had been walking away from the spot where he had last seen King Tobit.

"I'll see so much man-magic," Oban kept sighing. "Pix has told me about the box that you keep little people in, and they sing and dance and talk whenever you want them to."

"What?" Tam frowned. Then he

grinned. "Oh, that! It's called television. It's not that good really."

"And you can talk to people when they're somewhere else, with a little stick that you keep in your pocket."

"Mobile phones. Mum said I can have one when I'm older." Tam was beginning to cheer up. After all, he was going home. He was going to see Mum and Dad and Blue again. And it would be quite fun to show Oban all these gadgets. What would he make of his bike? he wondered. And aeroplanes, and cars?

"Mobile phones! We should have things like that here," Oban chuckled. "Such wonderful magic!"

Tam remembered what the Flame-reader had said. *We want no more of this meddling with mortals. We have our own magic here. Man-magic could destroy us. We have no need of it!*

"No, you'd ruin it!"

"Why? Why shouldn't we have it?"
Oban demanded.

"Because . . . because . . ." It was so
hard to explain. "Because what you've
got is better. And we can never have it
where I live, not your kind of magic,
not dream magic." Because that was
what it was. It didn't seem real any
more. Nothing seemed real. And the
words of the flame-reader were chiming
in his ears:

Find the boy Tobit, and take him home.
Will you do that? Never let him come here
again. Do you hear me? Do you promise?

But how could he keep his promise?
He had found Tobit and lost him again,
because of fairy trickery. He didn't
know how to play tricks like that.

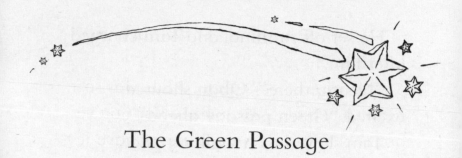

The Green Passage

The last bit of the journey was an exciting slippery scramble up one side of the glass mountain and a top-speed slide down the other. They were both shouting their heads off when they reached the bottom.

"Amazing!" Oban laughed. "You just can't do that when you're a king." He turned to Tam. "Aren't we having fun together! Race you!"

He set off running, and Tam charged after him.

"Nearly there!" Oban shouted, excited. "Green passage ahead!"

Tam slowed to a walking pace.

They were approaching the misty darkness of the cave that led to the green passage and home. He felt a lump in his throat. He hadn't said goodbye. He would never see his great-grandpa again, and he had never even said goodbye. When they entered the gloom of the cave they could just see a tiny pinprick of blue light at the far end. Tam knew it was the light of home.

The guardian of the cave came stumbling towards them, green-toothed and grinning, rubbing his cracking fingers together.

"Snix snee," he cackled, recognizing Oban. "Kingy-bye?"

"Yes, I'm going." Oban smiled. "King

Tobit will take care of you all now."

Then Tam saw shapes moving in the
darkness as all the sleeping soldiers
woke up and stretched and struggled to
their feet to salute the departing king.
Their long grey beards touched the

ground. It was the first time they had been awake for a thousand years, and their limbs were stiff and their old eyes blinked sleepily. They peered at Oban, trying to recognize him without his magnificent cloak.

"Seven more steps, and we'll be there!" Oban laughed.

Tam had never felt more miserable in his life. He put his hand in his pocket and felt his starburster. He put it to his eye and looked around. The blue light that showed through the crack in the boulders sparkled like jewels. He twisted the starburster round and now he could see the secret bower where the king and queen of Faery lived. He could see the queen sleeping in her hammock as it swayed gently backwards and forwards.

He moved the starburster again. He could see Morva and Pix, munching petals. And now, at last, he saw a little boy in a dazzling white cloak. He was

sitting cross-legged on a throne. Elfa,
the pretty fairy with purple eyes, was
hovering round him with bowls
overflowing with petals. The boy looked
up for a moment. His eyes were
shining. He gazed straight at the
starburster as if he knew he was being
watched. His lips moved, and although
Tam couldn't hear a word of it he knew
what Great-grandpa Toby was saying.

"Goodbye, Tam."

He put the starburster back in his
pocket.

"Ready?" Oban asked.

"Ready," said Tam.

Together they put out their hands
and touched the mossy green boulders.
With no effort from them at all, the
boulders swung apart. The brilliant blue
of day rushed to meet them. They
stepped forward and the boulders slid
together behind them without a sound.

They were home.

THE
WINDSPINNER

BERLIE DOHERTY

Illustrated by Lesley Harker

For Tommy and Hannah

Contents

This is what happened last time:

Oban, the king of the fairies, just loved Great-grandpa Toby's humming machine. It was really a harmonica, and sometimes it sounded wonderful, and sometimes it didn't, but he wanted it because he loved man-magic. He wanted it as much as he had wanted Great-grandpa Toby's starburster, which was really a kaleidoscope. He sent his fairy daughter, Pix, to bring Great-grandpa Toby and Tam to Faery, but she had to turn Great-grandpa into a nine-year-old boy to get him there. He was given a fairy name, Tobit, and was captured by Oban's mother, the fearsome Damson-hag. Tam found him with the help of the oldest fairy of them all, the terrifying Flame-reader. With the Blue Bear and Pix he rescued Tobit and locked the Damson-hag inside her own golden cage. At last they came face to face with King Oban, who made Tobit change places with him, and told Tam that he wanted to go back home with him and learn about man-magic.

The Secret

Tam had a secret. It was such a wonderful, exciting, strange, troublesome secret that he knew he had to share it with someone. All night he kept thinking about it, wondering whether he had dreamed everything that had happened, but as soon as it was daylight he could make out a strange blue light at the end of his bed. When the blue light grew stronger, it was just possible to make out a figure, shimmering so brightly that it hurt Tam's eyes to look at him. He knew it was Oban.

"So you really are here," he sighed. "I thought it was a magic dream."

"Don't tell anyone who I am," Oban

said. "I want to be a secret. Don't tell them anything about my kingdom."

"All right, but you mustn't let anyone see you," Tam said. "I can't pretend you're just an ordinary person, can I?"

They touched hands, and the blue light disappeared, but the air in Tam's room had a strange, fluttering kind of excitement about it, and Tam could tell that Oban

was still there.

But he knew it was going to be very hard, keeping such a huge secret from his parents. When he went downstairs for breakfast, he felt as if he was bursting, as if he had *I've got a secret* written all over his forehead, as if you only had to look into his eyes to know what it was. He very nearly told Mum, just before he went to school.

"Everything all right, Tam?" she asked, and he nearly blurted it out then and there, but Tam's little sister Baby Blue fell over and had to be comforted, and then the moment was gone, because Dad started asking if anyone had seen his lunchbox.

"I know I made my sandwiches last night," he said. "Lovely smelly stilton cheese sandwiches. And yours have gone too, Tam. What's going on?"

Tam knew very well what had

happened to the sandwiches. Well, he could answer that bit without letting any secrets out.

"I ate mine, and Great-grandpa Toby ate yours," he said.

"What, in the middle of the night?" Dad asked. "Whatever for?"

"Erm, we were hungry," Tam said. "But it wasn't last night, it was ages ago," and then he shut up, because he remembered that time was different in that other place he had been to. He rooted around in his school bag and brought out the two empty lunchboxes. He couldn't help smiling inside himself to think that they'd been

all the way to Faery and back.

"I'll have to make more, but there's no smelly stilton left," Dad grumbled. "And where is Great-grandpa Toby anyway? He's usually blowing that humming machine of his by now, the noisy old nuisance."

"He's out," said Tam.

"*Out?* Where out, at this time of the morning?"

Tam ran upstairs, feeling miserable. There was no way he could tell Mum and Dad where Great-grandpa Toby really was. They'd never believe him, and it was all part of the terrible, wonderful secret. They would probably never see him again either. How could he tell them that?

He could hear Mum running up the stairs to look in Great-grandpa's room. "His bed's not been slept in!" she shouted down the stairs. "He's been out all night!"

Tam flung himself on his bed. Spinner,

his little silver
spider who
had come
home
with him
from
Faery,
danced up to him across the pillow,
singing a sweet, comforting song. "Ssh!"
said Tam. "Don't let them hear you!"

Spinner curled up into a ball and
bobbed back up the lampshade, tucking
her silvery thread behind her as she did so.
Baby Blue crawled into the room, tugging
her favourite teddy along
with her. She propped
herself up into a
wobbly sitting
position and
pressed Teddy's
tummy.

"My word!"

Teddy growled, sounding just like Great-grandpa.

Mum rushed to the room. "Here he is," she called to Dad, and then stopped, staring around. "That's funny, I was sure I heard his voice then," she said.

Tam picked up Teddy in case Blue pressed his tummy again.

"No Great-grandpa here," he said. "Keep quiet," he whispered to the bear. When the fairy Pix had turned Great-grandpa Toby into a nine-year-old boy, she had left his voice behind in Blue's teddy bear, in case he ever needed it again. How could Tam tell Mum that all that was left of Great-grandpa Toby was his growly old voice? He didn't know where to start, so he didn't begin at all. He just frowned at Teddy and put him carefully on the shelf, well out of Blue's way.

"Get yourself ready for school," Mum

told Tam. She propped Blue up in the little baby chair that was kept in Tam's room so that they could listen to bedtime stories together. "I'll bath you in a minute, Baby Blue. I'm going to ring Great-aunt California to see if she's heard anything from him."

Blue chuckled up at Tam. Tam wondered if it counted, telling secrets to a baby who wouldn't understand, and who couldn't talk yet. She certainly wouldn't be able to pass the secret on. He decided to try. He had to tell somebody.

"Blue," he said. "Guess where Great-grandpa Toby is?"

As soon as he said that, the air around him shivered with hundreds of tiny blue sparks.

"You promised. You promised!" a voice thundered. Blue burped in fright as the strangest person she had ever seen appeared: a tall creature with wild silver

hair like the fluff on a dandelion, and eyes
like round golden suns. He was dressed in
a cloak that shifted and shimmered

from white to silver to blue and back
again.

"And you promised to keep hidden!"
hissed Tam. "Disappear, Oban!"

For a second the two glared at each

other, Tam and the glimmering stranger, and then Mum called up the stairs, "School, Tam!"

The stranger disappeared; Tam ran downstairs. Blue clapped her hands together, not knowing whether to laugh with wonder or cry with fright.

"My word," Teddy growled, all on his own on his shelf.

Back to School

It was bewildering for Tam to be back in the swirl of the schoolyard again. Apparently he had only been away from home for one night. No one had missed him, and yet so much had happened that he seemed to have been away for ages; weeks and weeks. He had had so many wonderful adventures and survived so many dangers, and all because of Great-grandpa Toby's humming machine. None of his school friends had ever been through anything like that, he was quite sure, and yet he had no way of sharing it with them. It was all part of the incredible secret. If only he could tell Shaz or Harry.

"What did you do last night?" he asked Harry.

"Watched telly, went to bed," Harry said.

"What did you do?" he asked Shaz.

Shaz shrugged. "Played a computer game with my dad."

Tam glanced round. "Ask me what I did," he whispered.

"All right. What did you do?" Shaz
asked.

"I can't tell you! But it was really
exciting," Tam yelled. He ran away and
the boys started chasing him, but they
were suddenly distracted by something
that was happening by the school gate

and they ran off in the other direction. One of the girls, Molly, was shouting to her friends, giggling about something that she had just seen. At that moment they were all called in for the end of break, and once again Tam had lost the chance of giving anyone a clue about his secret.

"What was all that about, Molly?" Mrs Ryan asked. "I could hear you shouting about something in the playground."

Full of excitement and importance, Molly told her that she had just seen a strange person peering through the railings.

"He was really weird," Molly giggled. "Really, really weird."

"A stranger?" Mrs Ryan said, frowning. "What was he like?"

"He had fluffy silver hair, and he was dressed in funny shiny clothes," Molly said. "He was a bit like a boy but he wasn't a boy really. Perhaps he was an angel."

Tam's heart started thumping. He knew exactly who it was. So Oban had followed him to school. Right, he thought, if Oban could break his promise, so could he. But everyone was laughing at Molly.

They all thought she was just making it up. If they didn't believe her, they were hardly likely to believe Tam if he said, "Oh, don't worry about him, he's just the king of the fairies." So he kept his head down and his mouth shut. He willed Oban to go back home and hide in his cupboard again.

Tam slid his hand into his pocket. Something tickled his fingers. He drew Spinner out, cupping his hand round her, then let her scamper across the table for a second or two before he scooped her up and put her back in his pocket again. He saw Molly watching him.

"Ask me why I've got a spider in my pocket," he whispered.

"I don't want to know," Molly whispered back. "I hate spiders."

But at last Tam found a way to tell someone his secret. The children had all finished the work they were doing on ancient monuments. Mrs Ryan said she was so pleased with them that they could spend the rest of the morning writing stories, while she sorted through a big parcel of books that had just arrived for the library.

The children took out their writing books and pencils. Tam gazed around him. He wasn't very good at writing stories. He tried to catch Shaz's eye but Shaz was already scribbling away, no doubt writing one of his usual fantasies about playing football for England even though he was only nine years old. Molly was staring dreamily into space. Harry was drawing a picture of a dragon. And then suddenly Tam knew what he could write about. He could write the most amazing story he had ever written, and it would all be true, every word of it. But he wouldn't be breaking his promise, would he? Surely words on a page didn't count as telling anyone. Mrs Ryan would be the only one to see it, and she would think it was just a made-up story.

Now it was his turn to scribble as fast as he could. His pencil scurried across the pages as if it had a life of its own. Every so often he was stuck for a word, and he gazed into space just as Molly had been doing. It was as if somewhere out there, in the sky outside the window, or on the wall, there was exactly the word he was looking for. The bell rang for lunch, the children tidied their books away on the shelves, and still Tam was writing.

"Finish!" Molly whispered to him, and

he ignored her – in fact, he didn't even hear her.

"I'm sorry to break into your writing spell" – Mrs Ryan smiled – "but it's time for lunch." She gently took his writing book away from him. "You're obviously inspired, Tam."

"But," said Tam, "I haven't brought him home yet!"

"Off you go," Mrs Ryan said. "I'm looking forward to reading this."

Tam followed Shaz and Harry out of the classroom. He felt a huge sense of relief. At last, at last, his secret was out.

The Secret Is Out

It wasn't until the very end of the school day that things started to go wrong again. Everybody was very busy designing the Christmas cards they would be making next week while Mrs Ryan was marking their work. At the end of the afternoon she looked up.

"Children, you've all been working really well. Would you like to hear a wonderful story to end your busy day? Put your things away and I'll read you something really, really good."

They didn't need to be told twice. If there was one thing all the children enjoyed, it was story time. They cleared their things away quickly and shuffled their chairs round to the story corner. Mrs Ryan wasn't holding a library book with a colourful cover; she was holding a pale blue writing book like the ones they all used in class.

"Are you ready?" she asked. They all nodded, sitting as still and silent as they could. They were as quiet as mice. Mrs Ryan would never begin a story until everyone was ready to listen. Stories are so special, she said, that she never wanted anyone to miss a single word.

"It's called, 'The Night the Moon Went Blue'," she said.

Tam gasped. It was *his* story! He bent down so no one would see his face. My story! he thought. Mrs Ryan thinks *my* story is wonderful. He felt a warm glow inside, a glow of pride and pleasure and embarrassment.

"*Last night the moon was blue*," Mrs Ryan read. "*My great-grandpa told me that anything can happen when the moon is blue,* and he was right. Guess what? A fairy called Pix came to our house, and something magic happened. She turned my great-grandpa into a boy who was only nine years old, and magicked him off to fairy land."

Everybody laughed.

"This is going to be a good story," Molly whispered to Tam. He nodded, his face hidden in his hands.

Mrs Ryan carried on reading. "Then Pix tried a few spells that went wrong. She turned me into a great-grandpa! I had whiskers on my chin and my voice was deep and growly."

Molly nearly fell off her chair, she was laughing so hard.

"But she was only a beginner fairy – she hadn't been doing spells for very long.

So she tried again. She managed to turn me back into a boy, but then she turned my baby sister into a great-grandpa!"

The children were all laughing so
much that Mrs Ryan could hardly carry

on. Tam lifted his hands away from his face and giggled happily.

"Shush, everybody, this is where it gets really exciting. Shall I carry on?" Mrs Ryan asked. Everyone settled down again to listen.

"*Then,*" she read, "*the wonderful thing happened. I was flying, really flying, through the blue stars and over the blue moon. I landed in Faery, the place where all the fairies and elves live. I had to find my great-grandpa. I had to rescue him and bring him home. But first I had to meet the terrifying Flame-reader. He is the oldest fairy of them all, and he is bent and twisted like a tree, with gnarly hands and knobbly fingers. He made me chop off his hands as if they were twigs, and throw them in the fire. They turned into pictures that told him where my great-grandpa was. He had been stolen by the Damson-hag. Sometimes she is like a beautiful girl, and sometimes she is so old and bent that her chin nearly touches the ground. She had trapped my great-grandpa inside a golden cage, and she danced to the music he played her on his humming machine. She is very wicked, and very dangerous. She is the mother of Oban, the king of the fairies."*

You could have heard a mouse breathe, it was so quiet in the classroom then. Everyone was listening with every bit of themselves. But at the sound of those words, "the king of the fairies", everything changed.

The air was suddenly alive with blue zigzags, as if the classroom was full of lightning. The window behind Mrs Ryan shattered into hundreds of pieces, drifting round her like coloured stars. And on the windowsill stood a figure with silver hair like dandelion fluff, and golden eyes, and a swirling cloak that shifted from white to

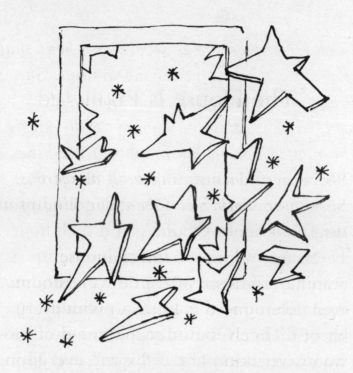

grey to silver to blue and back again.

"You promised!" Oban shouted. "You promised not to tell."

The House Is Pixillated

Nobody said anything at all about the broken window. Stranger still, nobody said anything about Oban. As if a spell had been cast over them, the children just stared at the spot where he was standing, and nobody said anything, nobody moved. Then Oban disappeared as if he had never been. The bell went, and Mrs Ryan brushed the coloured stars off her clothes as if she was just waking up from a dream. She sent the children to the cloakroom to fetch their coats, and then they all ran out into the yard to meet their parents. Mum was waiting for Tam, with Blue fast asleep in her pushchair. Tam rushed up to tell her that it really wasn't his fault, but Mum was in a hurry. There was no time to show her the broken window in the classroom. She wasn't in the mood for listening anyway.

"I've had such an awful day," she said. "For a start, Great-grandpa Toby is still missing. I've been ringing round all his friends and no one's seen him. And I've spent the rest of the day looking for things, and they've all turned up in the wrong places. The washing-up liquid was in the fridge, the milk was in

the bathroom, my shoes were in the waste-paper basket, and Blue's hat was on a grapefruit in the fruit bowl. The house is pixillated! You know what it reminds me of, don't you?"

Pixillated. Well, Tam had heard that word before. It was when Pix had lived with them instead of Blue, and she had done really naughty things like making the cupboards empty themselves just by looking at them, and the cuckoo clock shout "*cuckoo*" till it drove everybody crazy and Dad had shoved it in the bin.

"I had a good look at Blue to make sure that she hadn't been swapped for that horrible goblinny thing again," Mum went on. "But she's still my beautiful Blue, and you're still my lovely Tam, so nothing like that has happened, thank goodness. But something's going on. Look!"

They had arrived at the house, and could see even before they opened the door that the hall light was being switched on, off, on, off. The television blared out at just about the loudest it could possibly go. Blue woke up, screaming. Mum hurried to switch the television off. Now they could hear Great-grandpa's humming machine being played, very badly.

"So it's him! Great-grandpa Toby's back from wherever he's been, and playing silly tricks!" Mum said. She ran upstairs to Great-grandpa's room, but it was empty. Now the buzzy, jangly, tinny noise was coming from the bathroom, now the toilet, now the kitchen, now up and down the stairs. But wherever they looked, there was no sign of Great-grandpa Toby. There was no sign of anyone.

"You see what I mean?" Mum said. "The house is pixillated!"

She lifted Blue out of her pram, shushing her and cuddling her to calm her down. Tam went quietly up to his room and sat on his bed.

The house was silent now. He knew exactly what was causing all this noise and upset. He knew why, too. And he also knew that it couldn't go on any longer. He and Oban hadn't really discussed what was going to happen when Oban came home from Faery with Tam. All they had done was make a promise to each other: "I promise to keep it a secret, if you promise to stay hidden."

It had been so easy to say, but so hard to do. And it wasn't all Tam's fault either. If only Oban would stop playing tricks, things would be a lot better. He sensed that somewhere in his room Oban was watching him. It was time for them to have a proper talk.

"I know you're there," Tam said.

Nothing.

"There was no need to break the window."

Nothing.

"You just can't turn up at my school like that, all flashy and sparkly."

Still nothing.

Tam sighed. "It's no use sulking, Oban. It's not going to work. I can't hide you for ever. If you really don't want people to know who you are, you'll have to use your magic to make yourself look just like everybody else. Try to be a normal nine-year-old boy. Surely you can manage that."

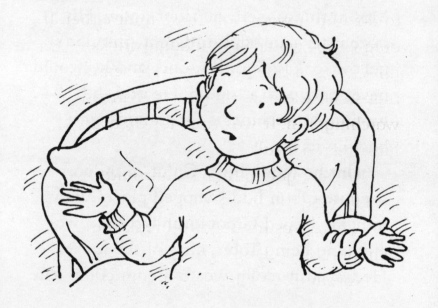

Still no word from Oban.

Tam sighed and lay on his bed, staring up at the ceiling. Spinner had hoisted herself up there again and was busily making herself a web in the corner. He liked having Spinner here. He'd always wanted a pet spider. As long as she didn't sing too loudly or shimmer too much, nobody else would notice her really. She would always be his now, to remind him of that amazing adventure he'd had. Mostly things were all right again. His starburster was back in Great-grandpa's yellow sock, safe and sound, and he would never part with it again. He had the humming machine, if Oban had put it back in its box.

But he didn't have Great-grandpa, because Oban had swapped places with him. He hoped Great-grandpa Toby was enjoying being Tobit, king of the fairies. He hoped it really was a dream come true for him. He tried to remember how his great-grandpa had looked when Oban had crowned him King Tobit, sitting proud and excited on the fairy king's horse. Was it really what he had wanted all his life? What would he be doing now? he wondered. He closed his eyes, imagining King Tobit swinging backwards and forwards in a hammock made of daisy chains. Backwards and forwards, backwards and forwards, always a child, always a nine-year-old boy. Was that what he really wanted?

Tam must have fallen asleep, because the next thing he was aware of was Dad whistling in the bathroom. He hadn't even heard him driving the car into the garage or running up the stairs to take his work clothes off. Next thing, Mum called up the stairs to tell Tam that tea was ready.

And when he went down to the

kitchen, the most surprising thing of all
the surprises that day was waiting for him.
Mum was putting food onto four plates.
Dad was sitting at the table already. Blue
was sitting next to him in her high chair,
chuckling. And a strange boy was pulling
faces at her.

"Sit down next to your friend," Mum
told Tam.

"My friend?"

The boy who was pulling faces at Blue
turned to look at Tam. At first Tam
thought he had never seen him before. He

was dressed in a pale grey sweatshirt and blue tracksuit trousers. His eyes were a light amber colour, not quite yellow, not quite brown. His hair was pale and very curly. He nearly looked like a normal nine-year-old boy, but not quite. There was something almost ghostly about the sheen of his skin. And when he smiled at Tam, a special, proud, secret smile, Tam knew for certain that it was no ordinary boy.

It was Oban, the one-time king of the fairies.

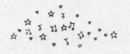

Spellbound

While they were eating, Mum chatted to Oban as if she had known him for years. Dad smiled at him and kept telling him to "Eat up, there's a good lad," and Blue chuckled and gurgled sweetly every time he looked at her.

He's charmed them, Tam thought. Enchanted them, just like the Damson-hag enchanted me. They think he's absolutely wonderful. They don't even want to know who he is, or anything about him, thank goodness. It must be his magic.

"Tam, you were right to invite Oban to stay here." Mum smiled. "He's such a lovely boy! But really, you should have told me. I'd have made a cake!"

"He doesn't like cake," Tam said. "He only eats flowers."

"Flowers! He seems to be doing pretty well with his mashed potatoes then!" Dad said. "Eat up, there's a good lad."

And it was true. Oban was tucking into mortal food as if that was what he ate every day of his life.

"Oban was telling me," Mum said, piling the fairy king's plate with carrots, "that his father lives ever such a long way away and his poor mother's in prison!" She helped Oban to some more gravy. "Poor child! And he has nowhere to live!"

"I know," said Tam. How could he say, *Well, he lives in a place called Faery, usually*? He had never even heard him mention his father before. Who could that be? he wondered. The father of the king of the fairies. That must be someone really powerful. Anyway, whoever he was, if he lived in Faery, he was just about as far away as anyone could be. Unless they happened to be a fairy or a nine-year-old boy and could get there by flying or just walking through a green passage that no one else could even see. And as for Oban's mother being in prison, well, that was true, in a way. She was the wicked Damson-hag. She was still tied up with Spinner's thread and locked in the golden cage where Tam and Pix and the Midnight Bear had left her. She had to be. Tam still had the golden key in his pyjama pocket. So it was all true, except that Oban wasn't a child at all. He was a fairy, and he was thousands of years old, but try explaining that to your parents and they'd just tell you to stop being silly and to "get on with your dinner, lad".

"So is it all right for him to stay here?" Tam asked.

"Of course it is!" Mum twirled the gravy spoon round her head, spattering

Dad with drops of gravy. He didn't mind, she didn't mind. They were spellbound; there was no other word for it. "He can stay with us as long as he wants."

It certainly made things easier for Tam, not having to wonder where Oban had flitted off to all the time. Dad brought the camp bed in from the garage and Mum

hoicked the mattress out of the cupboard
under the stairs. They made a bed for
Oban next to Tam's. Bedtime was fun.
They all listened to Blue's bedtime story,
and then, when she was put into her own
room, the two boys had a pillow fight and
giggled for a few hours. Oban told Tam
stories about the most terrifying monsters

in Faery. Tam told Oban stories about
dentist's drills that wouldn't stop drilling
and sharks that lived in the toilet. At last,
at long last, they fell asleep. Tam's final
thought was about school tomorrow.
Oban would be going with him, of course.
Mum would tell Mrs Ryan that he was
Tam's friend and she was looking after
him for a bit. But what on earth would
Mrs Ryan say about the broken window?

In fact, Mrs Ryan said nothing about the
window. She smiled sweetly at Oban and
said of course he could be in Tam's class.
She brought in another chair so they
could sit next to each other, and even
asked Oban if he was warm enough,
sitting near the window. And the window
looked just the same as ever; it must have
been mended during the night. There was
no sign that anything had happened, and
nobody even mentioned it.

"No bits of glass anywhere," Tam said to Molly, who couldn't take her eyes off Oban.

"Bits of glass?" she asked. "What from?"

"The broken window."

"What broken window?" Molly was staring at Oban very strangely. "I've seen him before," she said at last.

"You can't have done," Tam said. "He's not from round here. You must have dreamed about him."

Molly pulled a face. "Don't be daft. As if I'd waste my dreams on boys! Hope you haven't brought that spider in with you today."

"What spider?" Tam asked.

"You know very well. The one you had in your pocket."

"Me? Keep a spider in my pocket? You must have dreamed that as well."

Molly looked puzzled. Oban smiled at her and she dazzled a smile back at him. Oh well, Tam thought, there goes another one. Mum, Dad, Blue, Mrs Ryan and now Molly, all under Oban's enchantment.

Even though she was totally charmed by Oban, Mrs Ryan soon discovered that he hadn't a clue about reading and writing. His handwriting was nothing more than fancy squiggles on paper. His

spelling didn't exist. And he had no idea
what to do with numbers.

"Oh dear," she said. "Which school did
you go to before?"

"No school," said Oban.

"I thought as much. You might have to
move down to the reception class, Oban."

"I'll teach him," said Tam.

Mrs Ryan laughed. "That's very sweet,
Tam, but it's impossible. He's going to have
to start right at the very beginning."

"He's really quick," Tam said. "Can't I just try?"

He thought of how quickly Oban had learned to do things at home, things he had never seen before. Just by watching Mum and Dad in the kitchen he'd learned how to make toast, boil a kettle, set the washing machine going. It was as if these were things he'd been doing all his life.

The funny thing was that at first Oban treated them all as if they were impossible, magical tasks that had to be solved, just like the ones Tam had been set when he was in Faery. *Follow the white path. Look neither over your left shoulder nor over your right shoulder. Never turn back, whatever you may hear. When the ruby cockerel crows, look for the golden feather . . .* Those were the words the Flame-reader had said when he sent Tam off on his journey to seek the Damson-hag, and Tam had been frightened and puzzled, but he had done it. And that was how Oban had been, staring at the toaster as if it was some kind of monster that might jump off the kitchen shelf and gobble him up. But he had worked out how to do it and he had made the breakfast toast, squealing with delight when the toast jumped up out of the toaster's mouth.

"Please?" Oban asked.

"All right," Mrs Ryan sighed. "It's a shame to split you up when you're such good friends. Oban can stay in our class today, and you can teach him how to write his own name. That's a start, anyway. But tomorrow he'll have to go into the reception class with Mrs Hooley. Go and sit in the story corner with him."

Tam began by reciting the letters of the alphabet to Oban, just once. Oban thought for a minute in deep, solemn silence. Then he stood on the table and shouted, "Abcdefghijklmnopqrstuvwxyz," at the top of his voice, and all in one breath. Everybody clapped.

"Goodness," said Mrs Ryan, not even telling him off for standing on the table. "Well done."

"And this is how you write it," Tam said. He wrote the letters on a piece of paper. Oban looked at them once and copied them down on another piece, without even looking at Tam's page again.

Mrs Ryan was watching, her face bright with smiles. "Astonishing," she said.

"My name is Oban," Tam said, and wrote it down.

Oban stared at the paper. "My name is Oban, my name is Oban," he kept repeating, as if they were the most wonderful words in the world. Then he turned the paper over and wrote, *My name is Oban. Your name is Tam*, in beautiful, flowing handwriting, and with not one single mistake.

By this time Molly, Harry and Shaz was leaning across the desk following every movement of his fingers, as if he was a magician at a birthday party, and they were trying to find out how he did his card tricks.

"You knew already," Molly said. "You were pretending."

But Oban gave her such a hurt, angry look that she slid back into her chair, her eyes welling up with tears. "Sorry, Oban. It's just that you're so clever."

"Bet you can't spell my name," said Charlotte.

Without even asking her what it was, Oban wrote it down. Not only had he remembered the name of every child in the class from when Mrs Ryan read out the register, but now that he had learned to spell, he could write them all down.

"I told you he was clever," Tam said. "Shall we move on to numbers now?"

Mrs Ryan nodded and settled the class down. It was time for them to do some work of their own. She let Tam and Oban work together, just occasionally looking over Tam's shoulder to check what was going on, and smiling her approval. It was the best day Tam had ever spent at school.

By the end of the afternoon he had taught Oban everything he knew. Oban could even work the computer, flashing from one program to another, marvelling at the animations and sounds that came from it. "Wonderful man-magic," he kept muttering under his breath.

When they went into the hall for afternoon assembly, Oban watched Mrs Hooley playing a hymn on the piano. As soon as she had finished he slid onto the piano stool and played the same hymn from memory, and then closed his eyes and played something so spiralling and mysterious and wonderful that every child in the room held their breath. And by now, of course, there wasn't a single person in the school who wasn't utterly and completely enchanted by him.

The Wonder Child

It was amazing how soon word got out that there was a wonder child at Tam's school. Children told their parents, parents told their friends, and before long the journalists were at the door, cameras flashing. Mum said they were being a bit of a nuisance, but she was so proud of Oban that she wouldn't have dreamed of sending them away. She bought copies of every newspaper. OBAN, THE CLEVEREST NINE-YEAR-OLD IN THE WORLD, one of the headlines said.

Oban gazed in awe at his photograph in the papers. "How did I get there?" he kept asking. And then he would frown and say, "That's such good magic."

And there was more fame to come. He

was interviewed by the BBC outside school one day. He politely performed his latest trick of calculating how much electricity was being used by the Christmas lights in town, and then he counted the stars in the galaxy by simply staring up at the sky, which was only just beginning to grow dark. Then he raced Tam home to be the first to make toast. They sat on the settee together with Blue between them, feeding her jammy crumbs when Mum wasn't looking.

Later, after tea, Mum switched on the television news. Oban adored television. He thought all the little people lived inside it, and wondered if they ever managed to get out. And to his amazement, there he was on the news, being interviewed outside the school gates.

"It's me!" he shouted. "Me in the magic box!"

"Shush, Oban," Mum laughed. "I want

to hear what you're saying."

"But I'm still out here, I'm here!"
Oban shouted. He ran to the screen and
banged on it. "Get out!" he shouted. "Get
out!"

Mum and Dad were laughing so much
that their armchairs almost collapsed.
Even Blue was laughing, though she had
no idea what was going on. And suddenly
Oban turned round from the television
screen, his face nearly purple with fury.

"How dare you laugh at me!" he roared. *"Don't you know who I am?"*

The laughter stopped at once. Tam noticed that Oban's eyes were glowing with a fierce golden light. He seemed to be growing taller and his hair was turning silver. A blue light shimmered around him. Whatever spell he had cast to turn himself into an ordinary nine-year-old boy was wearing off. Without thinking twice, Tam

ran and turned off the lights. While Mum and Dad were fumbling about in just the flickering glow of the television screen, Tam grabbed Oban's hand and pulled him out of the door.

"Get upstairs, quick!" he whispered. "You're turning back into a fairy!"

Of course, Mum was upset. Tam told her that Oban had gone to bed early because he wasn't feeling himself, which was sort of true. Dad said it was no wonder he was behaving badly – it wasn't good for any child to have all that attention.

"No more journalists," he warned. "That lad's getting too big for his boots."

"That look he gave me!" Mum shuddered. "I've never known anything like it. He frightened me. His eyes seemed to burn right through me."

"He's a funny lad," Dad agreed. "They're all going on about him being

some sort of genius – how quickly he can
do things. Yet he thinks things like cameras
and televisions and cars are magic."

"He's not quite . . . normal," Mum
decided. "He was chewing a pot plant
before tea. You know, my Christmas
cactus! There's great bites taken out of all
the leaves now."

Tam crept out of the room and up the
stairs. Things were getting serious. Not
only was Oban turning back into a fairy,

but the charm he had cast over Mum and Dad seemed to be wearing off too. They didn't seem to like him any more.

"He's got funny eyes," he heard Dad saying. "I've always thought that. And his skin's a bit blue, isn't it? Shiny blue!"

Tam went into his room. Oban wasn't in his bed, or anywhere in sight. He looked for him in the bathroom and in the cupboard, and then he opened the window and looked out. It was too dark outside to see anything clearly, but he fancied there might be a bit of blue light moving about on the lawn.

"Oban!" he hissed. "Don't eat all the shrubs, will you?"

There was no reply.

Tam closed the window and sat on his bed. He opened the drawer in his bedside table and took out his humming machine, and played a little low, sad tune on it. The fun seemed to have gone out of having

Oban here now. For days he had enjoyed being Oban's friend, watching how he could astonish people with his amazing memory and skills. But what if he was really turning back into a fairy?

Things would be very different if he did. Oban in Faery hadn't been a funny boy who everybody loved. He had been a terrifying king, proud and fierce with the kind of magic that turned horses to stone and fairies into nightmares. He could do anything he chose, anything at all, just by wanting to do it. So far he had only used his magic to appear and disappear, and to charm people like Mum and Dad and Mrs Ryan at school. But what if he wanted to use his real, powerful fairy magic here? Where would it all end?

Tam thought about what the Flame-reader had said to him: *We have no need of man-magic here. We have our own magic. Man-magic could destroy us.*

And what would fairy magic do to mortals?

Or perhaps Oban really was losing his magic, and that was why he couldn't look like a nine-year-old boy any more. What if nobody liked him now? What would he do then? What would happen to him?

Tam put down the humming machine and picked up the starburster that he still kept snug inside Great-grandpa Toby's yellow sock. He hardly ever looked through it these days. It always made him think of Great-grandpa Toby, and he felt sad when he did that. He missed him so much. At least Mum and Dad weren't asking awkward questions about where Great-grandpa Toby was. Every time he was mentioned, Oban seemed to be able to work his enchantment and make them stop worrying.

But Tam sometimes felt afraid. He had made a promise to the Flame-reader and

he hadn't kept it. *Find the boy Tobit, and take him home*, the Flame-reader had ordered him. *Will you do that? Never let him come here again. Do you hear me? Do you promise?* And Tam had promised, but he hadn't kept his word. He had left Tobit in Faery.

He looked through the starburster and moved slowly around his room. He could see his bed and his books and posters bursting into tiny coloured fragments, just as they always did, but it didn't really interest him any more. He was too worried to enjoy it. He pointed it up towards Spinner, who was humming dreamily to herself, bobbing up and down on her thread.

"What's gone wrong, Spinner?" he asked.

She looped herself round and round, and as he watched her through the starburster, it was as if she had turned into sparkling fragments of golden wire, and she had lots of mouths all opening and shutting in song. But it wasn't Spinner's sweet singing voice he could hear, it was the voice of Oban.

"I can do anything, anything at all. I can make man-magic, I can break man-magic. I can do anything. I can make nightmares."

Tam must have shouted out in fright,

because the next minute Mum was in his room, hugging him.

"There, there, it's all right," she crooned. "It's all right, Tam, I'm here. You've had a little nightmare, that's all."

"Oban's going to destroy us!" Tam gasped, and Mum laughed.

"Oban's fast asleep – look, in his bed."

And so he was, tucked up with the old teddy that Tam let him borrow. He was smiling to himself as if he was having a lovely dream, and his hair was golden again, and his skin a pale sandy pink without a hint of blue.

"Too much excitement," Dad said, coming into the room. "We'll have no more television interviews, no more newspapers. We'll all settle down and have a lovely Christmas."

Christmas

And it *was* a lovely Christmas. Until Oban
discovered the windspinner, that is. Up
until then he had been as charming and
funny as ever. Mum and Dad forgot about
his strange behaviour. In fact, it was as if it
had never happened. They were under his
spell again, and it seemed he could do
nothing wrong.

Oban loved everything about the
build-up to Christmas at school. He
adored singing the carols. He helped to
make the manger in the classroom. He
was an angel in the nativity play.
He cheered with everyone else when
Father Christmas came on the last day of
term and gave everyone a book.

Then came the holidays – making

cards, wrapping presents, going shopping in town with Mum. Oban loved every minute of it. He enjoyed making the Christmas cake with Dad and helping to decorate the tree. He looked surprised when Mum produced a clothes peg with a frilly dress made of tissue paper and told him it was a fairy, but he didn't say anything to contradict her. He just smiled to himself and put it right on the top branch, just as Mum had told him. Then, when Mum wasn't looking, he cupped his hands in the air and the clothes-peg fairy flew down and whirled towards Blue. She started crawling backwards in astonishment. The peg fairy twirled prettily around the room then whizzed back up to her branch, a smiling bit of wood and tissue paper again. Tam wasn't quite sure whether it had really happened, but Blue was quite certain about it.

"Again, again," she kept shouting,

holding up her hands to the peg fairy on the tree.

On Christmas Eve Tam and Oban helped Mum to make mince pies. She made the pastry and then let Tam cut it into fluted rounds with the pastry cutter. He managed to cover his nose and his hair, his jumper and the kitchen floor with flour. Oban spooned Dad's home-made mincemeat into each of the pastry cases, licking the spoon whenever Mum wasn't looking. When the pies were cooking, the kitchen was filled with wonderful, sweet smells, and as soon as they were brought out of the oven the

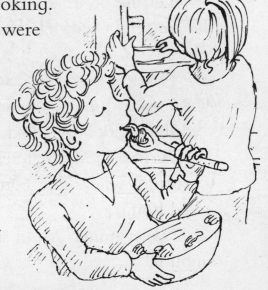

boys wanted to eat them. Mum made them wait until they were cool. "They'll burn your mouths!" she warned. "And you can only have one each, mind, and save the rest for tomorrow."

"And don't forget to put a couple on the doorstep for Father Christmas," Dad reminded them. "He's got a lot of work to do tonight; he'll be hungry by the time he gets here. I'll put a glass of sherry out for him too."

"Let me do it, let me!" Oban shouted, dancing about on his toes with excitement.

"Haven't you ever done this before?" Mum asked him.

Oban shook his head.

"Perhaps you don't celebrate Christmas where you come from?" Dad asked him.

"Never mind." Mum smiled. "Let him enjoy it."

"But why is Father Christmas so special?" Oban asked.

"Well, he's not like anyone else," Mum said.

"He's a bit of a magic figure," Dad said.

"He's a bit like the king of the fairies," Mum said, and for a second the kitchen was filled with a silence that was so big it was like a balloon full of air.

"We'll be going to church tomorrow." Mum broke the silence at last. "You'll like that, Oban. And then we'll spend most of the day eating, and you'll like that too. But first" – she held up a pair of laddered tights – "you must hang up your stockings." She cut the tights into two baggy legs, and gave them to the boys. "Blue will have to make do with one of Grandpa Toby's old yellow socks." She wiped her eyes with the back of her hand. "Where is he? That's what I want to know. I wish I knew!"

And then Oban smiled up
at her, and she smiled back at
him as if all her worries
about Great-grandpa Toby
had disappeared right out
of her head.

"What are these for?"
asked Oban, completely
mystified. He tried to put
the stocking on his leg.

"We hang them on
the bedposts for the
presents!" Tam
laughed. "Father
Christmas brings them.
Just wait and see!"

Blue was the first to wake up. Her yellow
sock was packed with things that rattled
and squeaked. Tam had some paints and a
torch, a model fire-engine and a bag of

marbles which he had to keep away from
Blue, a compass and a magnifying glass.
He thought they were all wonderful.
Oban had some of those things too, but he
also had a wand and a wizard's hat and
cloak, which puzzled him.

"You can be a wizard!" Mum said.

"Now you can do magic, lad!" Dad
said.

"Wear them," Mum said. "My, you
look like the real thing."

Oban wanted to please them so much
that he waved the wand about and made
some magic happen. Just little things at first,
like making a cupboard door open and
close when he pointed the wand at it or the
corner of the rug lift up and down again.

"Invisible string!" Dad grinned. "Well
done, lad. I used to do those kinds of tricks
myself."

Then Oban got carried away. He
swirled the wand at the Christmas tree

and made the little electric lights on it burn like real candles. He made Blue's fluffy animals stand up on their own and dance around her. And he turned the snow falling outside the window into hundreds of white butterflies. It all happened so quickly that it was almost as if it hadn't happened at all.

"I think I've had too much sherry!" Mum giggled. "I'm seeing things, I am."

Dad took off his reading glasses and rubbed them up and down on the jumper Mum had knitted for him. "That's better," he said, putting them back on. "For a minute I thought I was going la-la!"

"I think you'd better stop being a wizard for a bit," Tam whispered to Oban.

It was all very well doing pretty little tricks like that, but he knew that Oban could do something much more powerful if he felt like showing off. He wouldn't need a wizard's wand from the supermarket to do it either. He could feel a kind of thrill in the air, a kind of trembling around Oban, and it made him afraid.

"You can play with my magnifying glass instead if you like."

"Oh, that's much better," Oban said. He dropped the wand and held the magnifying glass up to Blue, so that when he looked through it, her face loomed towards him like a balloon. "Magic!" he laughed. "Real man-magic! How does it do that?"

After the presents came the meal. Tam and Oban set the table while Mum put the last touches to the vegetables and Dad stirred the gravy. Oban munched some holly to keep him going. He seemed to be able to eat as much mortal food as anyone else as long as he started off with flowers or plants.

"Doesn't that prickle you?" Tam asked.

"It tickled a bit," Oban admitted. "But it tastes delicious. Want some?"

Tam pulled a face and shook his head. "Don't eat the berries. They're poisonous."

"Even to fairies?"

"Shush!"

Mum bustled in with the roast turkey. Dad followed, carrying Blue, and they all sat down to their Christmas meal. Mum started crying straight away.

"I wish we knew what had happened to Grandpa Toby," she said, blowing her nose on her serviette. "I do miss him."

"He's always wandering off somewhere," Dad reminded her. "He cycled round the world when he was seventy-five, remember? It was the year we got married, and he never said a word to anyone about his plans. And only five years ago he went on a bus trip to China without telling anyone. He'll be back when it suits him." He piled turkey onto all the plates. "I think he'd fly to the moon if he had half a chance. And it's much quieter without him. Think of the shindig he used to make with that blessed harmonica. What did he use to call it?"

"His humming machine," Oban said. "I love to hear him play it."

Mum stared at him. "But you've never

even met him, Oban."

There was a queer silence in the room. Tam held his breath. Oban had gone too far this time. Blue looked from one to the other of them and started to sob.

"Tam's told me so much about Great-grandpa Toby, I feel as if I've known him all my life," Oban said. "I can imagine what his humming machine sounded like. I wish he was my great-grandpa too," he sighed. Mum leaned across the table and patted his hand.

"Talking of which," Dad said at last, "we've forgotten all about his Christmas present for Tam! He bought it for you the day before he disappeared, Tam. It's been in the shed for so long that it went clean out of my head."

"A present from Great-grandpa Toby!" Tam shouted. "Can I get it now?"

"No!" Mum and Dad both shouted at once.

"I've slaved in the kitchen all morning," Mum said.

"I've peeled all those sprouts," Dad said.

"So eat your dinner first," they both said.

It wasn't too hard, eating Christmas dinner. But as soon as the mince pies and brandy sauce were finished, and Mum and Dad and Blue all dropped off to sleep in front of the fire, Tam and Oban rushed outside into the back garden. It had stopped snowing. The sky was glassy blue and the air felt as sharp as needles. They ran to the shed, tussling to be the first to go in. There it was, leaning in the corner with a piece of shiny red Christmas foil draped over it. Tam pulled away the paper and gasped with delight.

"A new bike!" he breathed. "A really and truly brand-new bike! Oh, Great-grandpa Toby! If only he knew how much I wanted one. My old one is miles too

small now and it's gone rusty and the chain keeps coming off and Mum backed the car into it," he explained to Oban. "You can have it if you want. Oh wow! My new bike!"

He ran his hands lovingly up and down the shiny frame, pinged his fingernails against the spokes to make them trill, and wheeled the bike outside.

✾ 353 ✾

There was a silver and gold plastic windmill wired onto the handlebars, and a shiny bell with a picture of Dennis the Menace on it. Dangling from it was a note in Great-grandpa Toby's scrawly handwriting.

Happy Christmas, Tam. I hope you have many wonderful adventures with this windspinner.

The Windspinner from Great-grandpa Toby

"A windspinner!" Tam laughed. "Great-grandpa always has his own name for things." He swung his leg over the bicycle frame and cycled down the path, and back again, and down again. Even though there was snow on the ground, the covering was soft and light enough to ride on without skidding. He wheeled the bike out onto the pavement. There was no one in sight. It was as if all the world had fallen asleep after Christmas dinner.

"Let me ride it!" Oban ran out after him.

"No! It's mine! It's mine! It's all mine!" Tam shouted.

He rode off down the street, with

Oban running after him. They were both screeching with excitement.

"I can go to school on it! I can go down the park, and round the lake, and everywhere in the world on it! I can ride it to America and see Great-great-aunt California!" Tam laughed. "I love it! I love my windspinner! Yee-hah!" he yelled, sticking his legs out. "I'm flying!"

When he came back, Oban was waiting for him exactly where he had left him. "Now it's my turn. My turn! My turn!" he shouted.

"OK, OK," Tam said unwillingly. He wheeled the bike back into the garden. "Just in here. And very slowly, in case you fall off and scratch it."

It was just as well that he thought of that. Oban had no idea how to ride a bike. He couldn't get the hang of it. He couldn't balance, he couldn't make the wheels turn round, he couldn't even sit on it properly. All he could do was wobble, teeter to one side, and fall off. At first he thought it was funny; they both did. Tam was obviously anxious about his bike and kept his arms out ready to catch it as it fell yet again.

But after a bit, Oban started getting angry. If he tried once he tried a hundred times, and never succeeded in turning the pedals without falling off.

"That's enough," Tam said.

Oban picked himself up again and rubbed his elbow. "No. Another go."

"I'm getting cold," Tam said as Oban fell off again.

"Just one more try," Oban insisted.

"Let's go in." Tam caught the bike by its handlebars.

"No! No! *No!*" Oban screamed. "Teach me the magic! Teach me the magic!" He flicked the plastic windmill to make it turn, but it just did one rotation and then stopped.

"It's easy. It's just balance. All of a sudden you'll get it, and you'll never fall off again. But please let me have the bike back, Oban. You'll break it. You can have my old one – you can fall off that as

much as you like!"

Tam ran to the garage and wheeled
out his old bike. You could tell by looking
at it that it was too small for Oban, and
anyway, the frame was a bit bent where
Mum had backed the car into it.
Meanwhile, Oban was still falling off the
new one and getting more and more
furious with it.

"*Make the magic work!*" he roared. "I command you!"

Mum came out into the garden then – just in time to see Oban's fierce golden eyes burning into Tam. His skin was shimmering with a strange silver-blue light.

"Oban," she said, with a tremble of fright in her voice. "Stop that at once. And

I want to know who you really are, and where you've really come from."

But Mum didn't find out, because the blue light went out and Oban simply vanished, just as if he had never been.

Vanished

Christmas Day was very quiet after that. Dad washed the dishes, Tam helped to dry them, Blue woke up and played with her toys. Tam had tried to tell Mum the whole story, but she wouldn't believe any of it and told him to stop being silly.

"King of the fairies, indeed! He's got funny ways, that child. We did our best for him, but I've had enough. If he turns up again, I'll hand him over to the authorities, Christmas or no Christmas. He's a very clever little boy but we should never have bought him that wizard's outfit. He's gone too far this time. He frightened the life out of me when he lit up like that and did that vanishing trick. Pff! He probably used some kind of firework to make that blue light. But king of the fairies! No, I don't believe that."

"Mum, if you want to know anything about Oban, you've got to believe in magic. Real magic," Tam said.

And Mum laughed. "There's no such thing. Now, tell me honestly. Where did you meet him?"

So Tam stopped trying to explain about the green passage that led to Faery. He simply said that Oban had followed him home from the park one day. Mum found that easier to believe.

"He's a waif and stray," she said. "Poor little mite. Well, I'm worried about him, I am. No child should be left to wander around on his own like that. If he doesn't turn up soon, I think I'd better tell the police."

Oban's enchantment must be wearing off, Tam thought, worried. Mum had never mentioned telling the police about him before. And if she does tell them, they might ask me all sorts of questions that I can't answer.

When Tam went up to bed that night, he half expected to find Oban tucked up and fast asleep in the bed next to him, as if nothing had happened. But he wasn't there. The room felt very cold and quiet without him. Could Mum be right after all? Was there no such thing as magic? Maybe it was something that only children and Great-grandpa Toby believed in. He knew that only nine-year-olds could go to Faery. Did that mean that when he was ten, all the magic would go, and he'd never believe in it any more? But he was going to be ten next week!

Spinner bobbed down from the ceiling and tucked herself into the palm of Tam's hand.

"Spinner!" Tam laughed. "Of course there's such a thing as magic! I went to

Faery, didn't I?
That's where
I met you!
But what's
happening?
Where's Oban
gone?"

    And Spinner
sang in her high,
spirally voice,

"*Away and afar, away and afar,*
Burst the heart of the bluest star."

"I don't understand," said Tam.
She sang again:

"*Away and afar, away and afar,*
Burst the heart of the bluest star."

"Burst a star? Can I do that?" And
then Tam realized what Spinner meant.

"Of course I can!"

He went to his drawer, took out the starburster and ran to the window. The sky was brilliant with stars, like a field of crystal flowers. Now he could see that they weren't all silvery white. Some of them were tinged with colour, glowing blue like sapphires. He knew that colour well. Sapphire stars meant magic. The stars had been sapphire the night Blue was stolen. They had been

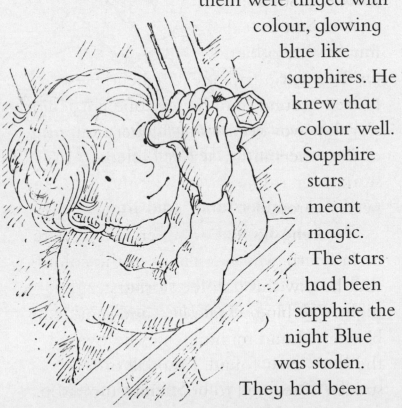

sapphire the night
Great-grandpa
Toby changed
into a nine-
year-old boy
and was taken
to Faery. Sapphire
stars meant that the
fairies were about.

Tam felt a fizz of excitement. He
looked around until he saw one particular
star that was brighter and bluer than any
of the others in the sky. He lifted up the
starburster, trained it towards that star, and
peered through it.

Nothing he had ever seen before, here
or in Faery, was as brilliant as the colours
that he saw through the starburster that
night. The blue star flashed and sparkled,
blossomed and fountained as he twisted
the starburster round. Then, all of a
sudden, it seemed to break into a million

shards that splintered in a shower of blue sparks. He had burst the heart of the star!

Now he knew that he was looking straight into Faery. The picture he could see wasn't split up into little coloured fragments any more, as it usually was when he looked through the starburster. It was as if he was looking through a window into another world: the world of the fairies. He could see the fields of flowers where the babies were nursed by Tanta, and where the fledglings stumbled and tottered, trying to spread their tiny stubs of wings. He saw the graceful, butterfly dancing of the older children. He could look even closer. Elva was there; laughing, teasing, purple-eyed Elva, and other children that he recognized. He could see Morva and the other little green elves. He saw the dark forest of soldier trees, and swooped as if he was flying over the Flame-reader's cave. He saw the

emerald forest and the glass mountains,
and the secret tower of the fairy king.
Now he could come in closer still. There
was Pix!

"Can you see me, Pix?" he shouted.

But no. Although
she turned her head,
although she
seemed to be
looking right at
him, she didn't
speak or show any
sign that she knew
he was there. She
had never even said

goodbye to him. The last time he'd seen
her was the day Great-grandpa sat on the
king's horse. What a beautiful horse it was,
with its golden mane and its tail crusted
with jewels. How proud Great-grandpa
had been. The new king! "Hail, King
Tobit! King of the fairies!" Pix had
shouted, and had run behind him, yelling
and cheering with the others, with never a
backward look at Tam, her mortal friend.

"Pix, Pix, I miss you," Tam whispered,
but she turned her head away.

Tam moved the starburster round so he could follow where she was going. Now she was in the queen's bower. A little boy lay fast asleep in a hammock. Surely it was the boy-king Tobit. Two sandy-haired children were rocking him gently backwards and forwards, backwards and forwards. It all looked very peaceful, full of sunshine and flowers. Tam twisted the starburster again. Now he could hear as well as see. He could hear someone singing, and recognized the voice of the queen of the fairies. She was sitting on her swinging throne, combing her drifting white hair.

"How beautiful she is," Tam said.

He moved the starburster again and watched Pix creep up to Tobit and shake his shoulder to wake him up. He yawned lazily and turned over in his hammock.

"Shall I go on with the story?" Tam heard Pix say.

"Mmm . . ." Tobit murmured sleepily.

"I was telling you about brave Prince Tamlin, and how he faced the Flame-reader in his cave."

"Oh yes. My word, it's very exciting," Tobit said. "Go on. You'd got to the bit where the Flame-reader said he was going to turn you into a slug." He giggled.

"That's not funny, King Tobit. Don't you understand how frightening he is?"

"Sorry."

"And then he told Prince Tamlin that he would turn him into a tree: 'Your bones will turn to wood, your blood will turn to sap, your toes will root you to the ground.' That's what the Flame-reader told him."

"That's not very nice," Tobit said. "My poor little great-grandson!"

"And then," said Pix, "the wonderful thing happened. The Flame-reader told Tamlin he *could* do all these things, because he was so powerful, but he wouldn't. Because although Tamlin wasn't a real fairy prince, he was as brave as anyone the Flame-reader had ever—"

Pix stopped suddenly. The fairy queen stopped singing. She held the jewelled comb clasped tightly in her hand. The two sandy-haired children stopped swinging the hammock and stared at one another, terrified.

"What's happening?" Tobit asked.

There was a loud stamping. Someone was marching heavily up the glass stairs. A figure strode into the hall; a huge, heavy figure with gnarled hands and shivering hair like autumn leaves, and deep, deep black eyes.

"How dare you!" he roared.

And far away, peering through the starburster, Tam recognized the voice at once. It was the voice of the oldest fairy of them all; oldest, wisest, most terrifying and most powerful. It was the Flame-reader.

The Flame-reader

Tobit slid out of the hammock and bowed deeply. Tam could see that his knees were trembling.

"Welcome, oldest fairy of them all!"

The Flame-reader ignored him completely. He snatched the comb out of the queen's hands and crushed it to splinters.

"How dare you let King Oban leave Faery!" he roared.

"It was not in my power to stop him," the queen murmured. She looked so small and frail next to the huge figure of the Flame-reader.

"Don't you know that he doesn't have the power to return?" the Flame-reader demanded. "Already his magic is reduced

to fancy party tricks to make mortals
laugh. He can never come back to us. He
will wander for ever on the other side of
the green passage, neither fairy nor
mortal. He can't die, like mortals can.
Thousands and thousands of years from

now he will still be wandering there, without friends or family, playing with the toys that men make, the baubles and tricks that he calls man-magic. A freak, they will call him. A clever freak. They will love him and hate him, but they will never understand him. He is not one of them, and never will be, though he will live for all time! And soon, soon, he will lose his magic for ever, his real magic, his fairy magic."

"Is there no way of helping him?" Tobit asked. His voice sounded small and scared after the roar of the Flame-reader's. The Flame-reader didn't even turn round to look at him.

Pix slipped out from her hiding place and crept on her hands and knees to Tobit. "Don't ask him questions!" she whispered. "He never answers questions."

Tobit ran to the Flame-reader and stood squarely in front of him. "My lord," he began, "oldest fairy of them all . . ."

The Flame-reader glared down at him.
"You have no place here," he roared. "This
is not your world. The other mortal boy
was told to take you home. He promised!"

"It's my fault," Tobit said bravely.
"I wanted to stay here. And King Oban
wanted me to swap places with him."

"*Ha!*" The Flame-reader
tipped back his head and
roared with laughter.
"*You!* Change places
with the mighty
king of the fairies!
Look at you! A
skinny little mortal
boy! I could turn you into a beetle, and
squash you under my foot!"

"Please don't!" Tobit's voice was
shaking. "I want to help, if I can. I want to
help Oban to come back."

"*You* help him? *You?*"

"I could try."

"He can't come back. Even if he wants
to, he can't come back," the Flame-reader
shouted. "Only one person can call him
home again. And that person is his
mother."

"The Damson-hag?"

"Yes. The Damson-hag. And where is

she? Locked in a golden cage without a key, her arms and her legs bound with the silk of a spider, and her mouth gagged with silver stitches that can never be broken, not with any spell, not with any magic. The spider who sewed the thread must unsew it, and where is she? How can King Oban's mother call him home? Tell me!"

"I d-don't know . . ." stammered Tobit.

"I can't free her, and you can't free her. Only the spider can do it. I don't have the spider, I don't have the key. I don't have the power. You should never have come here, you and your meddling boy Tamlin. It is not your place. You have only brought harm; great, great harm to Faery!"

And with that, the Flame-reader threw his cloak of rustling leaves round his shoulders, and left the secret bower of the fairy king and queen.

Tam put down the starburster. He was

very afraid; afraid for his great-grandpa,
afraid for Oban. When he picked it up
again, the blue stars had spun away. Black
clouds hung over the moon. The night was
completely dark.

"Oh, Spinner!" he sighed. "What can
we do?"

The Shepherd's Wheel

Boxing Day passed, and there was still no sign of Oban. Somehow all the Christmas lights and baubles lost their sparkle. Even the presents weren't fun any more. Tam rode his new bike up and down, up and down the street where he lived. The little windmill on the handlebars zizzed round, buzz-buzz, faster and faster as he picked up speed. He jingled his Dennis the Menace bell every time he approached anyone. Neighbours stopped and said, "What a lovely bike! I bet you got it for Christmas!"

He should have loved all that, but he didn't. He kept thinking how excited he and Oban had been when they first saw the bike in the shed, with the note from Great-grandpa Toby: *I hope you have many wonderful adventures with this windspinner.* He remembered how desperately Oban had wanted to ride the bike, and how at first he had teased him with it. How funny it was when he let Oban have a go at last and he kept falling off. But now he wished he hadn't made Oban so angry. If Oban hadn't been shouting, Mum wouldn't have come out of the house, and he wouldn't have run away.

More days passed, and still there was no sign of Oban. Tam had thought at first that he had gone straight back to Faery, but now he knew that wasn't possible. There was no way for him to get back there unless the Damson-hag wanted him to. And how could she say what she wanted, or anything at all, when she was all wrapped up in Spinner's thread?

Meanwhile, strange things were beginning to happen; unexplained, mysterious things, all over the country. The newscasters on television were excited about them. The grown-ups puzzled over them. Nobody could understand them. The first thing happened the day after Boxing Day, when the motorways were full of cars taking families back home after their Christmas holidays. For five whole minutes every single car on the road went backwards instead of forwards. People who were interviewed about it afterwards said it was the most frightening experience of their lives.

"Couldn't do anything about it," they said. "Good job it happened to everybody else on the road, or there'd have been collisions all over the place."

The next day, all the phone wires seemed to get tangled up. Mum got a phone call from a lady in Australia who wanted to buy a kangaroo, and when Dad tried to phone his friend to arrange a game of darts, he was answered by someone who thought he was ordering sausages. It was funny at first, but people started getting annoyed and worried, especially when they were trying to phone the emergency services. The lady next door phoned for an ambulance because she'd trodden on a hibernating hedgehog, and got the Chinese takeaway instead. And so it went on. When people switched on their electric lights, they heard "Rudolf the Red-nosed Reindeer" being played, and the light bulbs all flashed red. Tomato ketchup came out of the bathroom taps.

And every time something like that happened, there was the sound of tinkling laughter.

"It's the government's fault," some people said.

"It's global warming that's causing it," others said.

Tam knew very well what was causing it.

Oban was messing about with man-magic.

New Year's Eve came. The air was cold and sharp, the sky was a brilliant blue. The world seemed to have stopped turning, as if there was no breath left, as if it was waiting for some amazing thing to happen. Tam was restless. In two days' time he would have his tenth birthday, but he didn't feel at all excited about it. He didn't know what to do with himself. He asked his mum if he could ride his bike in the park, and she said it was a good idea.

"Get some fresh air, and maybe you'll stop fidgeting," she said. "I'll come with you. Blue can feed the ducks."

Tam decided he would cycle slowly with them and then race round the park on the special cycle path. But when he went to get his bike out of the shed, something was different. The bike was lying on the floor instead of being propped against the shed wall. The little windmill was upside down in a flower pot. He wheeled the bike out and inspected it for scratches. The same thing had happened yesterday, and the day before that. The bike was never quite where he expected it to be. It seemed to have been moving around in the night.

"What's the matter?" Mum called. "Aren't you coming?"

Tam shrugged and decided to say nothing about it. He wheeled the bike down the road behind Mum. Was he imagining it, or did he hear strange, high laughter in the air? He kept looking round, but there was no one to see. And yet he had the prickly feeling that he was being followed all the way down past the playing field and the swings, and right down to the duck pond. And then the feeling stopped, as if he was free again. As if something had let him go. It was weird.

Blue loved the ducks. When they lifted themselves up and beat their wings noisily across the pond, she shrieked with excitement and waved her arms up and down. She reminded Tam of Pix when she was learning to fly, flapping her stumpy little wing stubs, desperate to lift herself off the ground and join the flying fairies.

Blue got so excited that she needed a nappy change, so Mum wheeled her off to the ladies' toilets to sort her out. While she was doing that, Tam did his fast circuit round the park. He knew exactly where he wanted to go: to the Shepherd's Wheel, where the river flowed so fast over boulders that it could make an old millwheel spin round. He used to love going there with Great-grandpa Toby.

And that was where he saw Oban. He couldn't believe it. He had given up hope of ever seeing him again, and there he was, sitting with his back to him on one of the rocks in the river. He was unmistakable: his hair glowed with a silver light, and his clothes shimmered with a strange colour that Tam had never seen before. He was

close to the millwheel, watching it spin round and send up spirals of spray. He seemed fascinated by it, sometimes lifting up one of his arms and moving it round in a circle. He was copying the way the wheel was turning, in exactly the same way that Blue copied the ducks flapping their wings.

Tam decided to surprise him. Carefully he swung his leg over the bike frame and lowered it down onto the grass. He crept across to the river bank on tiptoe. His footsteps were almost silent on the grass, but suddenly Oban seemed to sense he was there. His whole body stiffened, as if he was listening out with every nerve to what was happening behind him. Then, just as Tam reached the river bank, Oban became as transparent as water. Tam was looking right through him at the boulder and the spinning water-wheel. Oban had disappeared.

Tam swung round quickly, and was just in time to see his bike, his precious bike, being raised up and then moving away at full tilt down the path all on its own. People jumped out of its way and then stared after it in amazement.

Now it was Tam's turn to be angry. "Hey, come back!" he shouted. "Bring my windspinner back!"

The bike wobbled and fell over, luckily onto grass. Tam went sprinting after it, and reached it as Mum and Blue came towards him.

"Tam, are you all right?" Mum called. "Did you fall off?"

"No, I didn't!" he said indignantly. He stared around. No sign of Oban, of course. He decided it was best not to mention him to Mum. It would only upset her. "Some kid pinched my bike, but I chased after him and he fell off it and ran away." It was nearly true.

"Ob boo whiz *whiz*!" Blue shouted, waving her arms again. Tam turned quickly, in time to see what she had seen. There was his plastic windmill floating all on its own, spinning in the wind, just as if an invisible person was running away with it.

Tam pushed the bike home so he could walk alongside Mum and Blue. Blue thought it was great fun to take off her mitts and throw them out of the pushchair, so Tam's job was to scoop them back up, pretend they were flying ducks, and tuck her hands back into them. It was hard work, wobbling the bike along with one hand.

"Stop it, Blue! No more!" he warned, and she giggled and threw her mitts on the ground again.

As they were coming up their street, they could see a large bundle of purple fluff on their doorstep, with a patched suitcase next to it.

"Goodness, what's that?" Mum asked. "Have the bin men dumped something on my step?"

The bundle of purple stood up, and they both said at once, "Great–great–aunt California!"

Now the fun will start again, Tam thought.

Great-great-aunt California

Great-great-aunt California was the next best person to Great-grandpa Toby. His little sister, as he called her, although she was nearly as old as he was. She only came to see Tam's family twice a year, because she had gone to America when she was sixteen years old to be a movie star, and had lived there ever since. Tam loved her nearly as much as he loved Great-grandpa. He jumped on his bike and raced down the road to meet her, jingling his bell wildly.

"Jeepers creepers, I love your bike!" Great-great-aunt California greeted him, flinging her arms round him and nearly knocking him off.

"It's my windspinner from Great-grandpa Toby," Tam said.

"A windspinner? Hmm. Are you sure? I might have a go on it later."

Mum had joined them by now. "California, why didn't you let me know you were coming? I wouldn't have gone out. You must be frozen."

"No, I'm not cold," Great-great-aunt California said. "Bought myself a new coat in the sales in town and I feel as warm as a bear in it. No, not a bit tired either. Only been waiting about an hour – that's no time at all. Just thought I'd pop along to see if there's any news of that dippy big brother of mine. Where's he shamoozled to this time, for cripe's sake? Know something about it, Tam? Jeepers creepers, I bet you do!" she whispered.

She followed Mum into the kitchen and sat holding Blue, cooing and cuddling her and smothering her with noisy kisses, while Mum made her a cup of tea. When

she'd eaten three mince pies and a slice of
Christmas cake, she stood up and winked
at Tam. "Now, young man, I reckon the
time has come for you and me to go up
to your room. You can show me all your
Christmas presents."

But although she clucked and gushed
over the magnifying glass and the fire-
engine, it wasn't Christmas presents she
wanted to talk about really. It was Great-
grandpa Toby. Tam kept her off the subject
for as long as he could. They even had a
great game of marbles on the bedroom
floor. She was a really good shot. But at
last she stood up, stretched her old bones
back into place, and then plonked herself

down on the bed so heavily that Teddy took a flying leap off the pillow and landed on the carpet.

"My word!" he growled.

Great-great-aunt California bent down and picked him up, staring at him.

"Jeepers creepers. If this didn't look like a raggedy tattered old teddy bear," she said, "I would think it was my big brother Toby. It isn't, is it?"

"No," said Tam. "It's a teddy bear."

He could feel Spinner wriggling about in his pocket. He put his hand in to keep her there, but she scrimped herself out between his fingers and scrambled up his wrist. Then she scampered up the wall to her corner of the ceiling, singing sweetly to herself,

"Silver and gold, silver and gold,
All is well when the story's told."

Great-great-aunt California leaned her head back, watching as Spinner busily made a web for herself. "My, oh my," she said softly. She looked back to Tam. "If I didn't know better," she said, "I'd say that was a singing spider. It isn't, is it?"

"It is," said Tam.

"Well, jeeps!" Great-great-aunt California whistled. "I've lived till I'm nearly ninety years old, and I've never met

one of those before.
I've seen the Seven
Wonders of the World,
and I've never come
across such a thing. I've
spent nearly all of my grown-up days in
America, and that sure is a wacky old
place, where all kinda 'mazing things
happen. But I've never seen or heard a
singing spider. Tell me, Tam" – she lowered
her voice to a scratchy whisper – "is
something magic going on here?"

"Do you believe in magic, Great-
great-aunt California?" Tam asked.

She roared with laughter and slapped
her thigh. "Believe in magic? You bet I
do!"

So Tam told her the whole story. It took a
long time. He was still talking when the
sky turned silvery dark and a tiny blue
star appeared, just to the left of the moon.

He began by showing Great-great-aunt California the shiny box with green velvet lining. "This is my humming machine," he said, opening up the box and stroking the harmonica.

"My, oh my, it's as good as apple pie!" she said. "Can I have a go?"

Great-great-aunt California was a much better harmonica player than her brother was. She closed her eyes and played some lovely old camp-fire tunes, nice and softly. Spinner bobbed down and swayed backwards and forwards on the end of her thread, singing along to the music.

Then Tam brought out the yellow sock, and showed her the kaleidoscope. She peered through it, whistling with joy and twisting it this way and that to make the colours in the room burst inside it. She ran to the window and swivelled the starburster round to look at the garden and the cold blue sky, the bare branches of the trees, and the starlings settling down for the night.

"Ain't the world a mighty fine place?" she marvelled. She lowered the starburster at last. "Well, I love that humming machine, and I love the starburster. But they ain't magic, Tam."

"Yes they are," Tam said. "They're
man-magic." And then he told her about
his adventures with the fairies – about
Oban, the king of the fairies, who loved
man-magic so much that he swapped
Blue for a goblinny little fairy-baby called
Pix. He told her how the only way Tam
could swap them back again was to give
King Oban the starburster. And then how
Oban turned Great-grandpa Toby into a

nine-year-old boy and kidnapped him just so he could get the humming machine. And he told her all the bits in between.

"And then, in the end, King Oban swapped places with Great-grandpa Toby so he could come home with me and play with man-magic for ever," Tam went on. "And now I think he's after my windspinner."

"Wait a minute, wait a minute." Great-great-aunt California waved her plump arms to interrupt Tam. "Let me get this straight. Oban swapped places with Toby?"

"Yes. He's called Tobit, and he's still there, and he's king of the fairies."

"He's *what*?" Great-great-aunt California shrieked. "He's king of the fairies?"

"Don't you believe me?" Tam asked.

"Of course I do! Jeepers creepers!" She wiped her eyes with the back of her hand.

"Ain't that cute! When he was a kid, that was all he ever wanted, and now he's gone and done it! OK. So what else is there to know? What's this gold and silver thing that your spider was on about?"

So Tam told her about wrapping the Damson-hag up in silver thread and locking her in the golden cage. He took the golden key out of his pocket and his great-great-aunt nursed it thoughtfully for a bit, then handed it back to Tam.

"You take good care of that," she warned. "We're going to need it."

Tam beamed at her. *We* was a wonderful word to hear. It meant that he didn't have to worry all on his own any more.

"What are we going to do, Great-great-aunt California?" he asked.

"Well, for a start, I suppose we could drop that mouthful and you could just call me Aunt California. That 'great-great' bit makes me feel about a hundred years old, and, jeepers, I ain't there yet. Say, why don't you let me have a chat with that teddy bear?"

"He doesn't say much," he said, handing Teddy to her.

She pressed Teddy's tummy.

"My word!" he growled.

"Oh boy!" she giggled. "That's so cute! Now, Tam, let's be serious. Did you tell me you've seen my brother in this Faery place, through the starburster? Let me have a look again. I want to know what he's up to, I sure do."

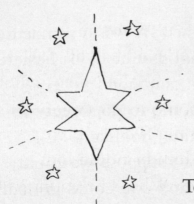

She took the
starburster again
and swizzled it
round. "Nope,"
she said. "I see
your lovely room,
Tam, and it's all
spangling with colour.
But no fairy palace."

Tam went to the window and looked
out. The sky was nearly dark now.

"Great-gr— I mean, Aunt California!
There's a blue star up there, just by the
moon. See it? Look at it through the
starburster. It might work."

Aunt California leaned out of the
window and swivelled the starburster at
the blue star. She gave a start, and then a
deep sigh.

"Jeep, jeep, jeep," she murmured, with
the starburster pressed to her left eye.
"There he is — my brother, but he's a kid

again! I don't believe it! What an
awesome place he's at! And he's all dolled
up in sparkly clothes – hey, but guess what
– I can see his stripy red pyjamas
underneath! My, oh my! There's pretty
kids bobbing round him bringing him
food – are they *fairies*? What's he eating?
Flowers! Bowls of flower petals! Oops – he
just gave an almighty burp, and I'm
not surprised!
Oh, but Toby,
Toby . . . !"
She lowered
the starburster
and turned
to Tam. "Do
you know
what? I think
he's crying!"

She handed the
starburster to Tam,
but the blue star

had faded to pale white again, and although it was bursting with brilliant colours, it wasn't showing Faery any more.

"Do you know what I think?" Aunt California sat down heavily on the bed again. "My brother is scared! We've got to get him home."

The Search for Oban

Tam and his great-great-aunt stared gloomily at each other.

"Show me that windspinner of yours again," she said at last. "But just for the moment, don't tell your folks what you've told me."

"They wouldn't believe me anyway," Tam said. "I tried to tell Mum once. They don't believe in magic."

"Humph," Aunt California said. "That's their problem."

They crept downstairs together. Mum was in the kitchen preparing tea. Dad and Blue were dozing in front of the fire. Tam and Aunt California let themselves out and went round to the shed, and Tam wheeled out his bike.

"Boy, oh boy," Aunt California said. "It sure is a beautiful bike, Tam. But d'you know what? It's not a windspinner."

"Great-grandpa's note said it was," said Tam, but she wasn't listening to him. She swung her leg over the frame and sat on the bike, and pedalled towards the street. "You can run behind," she shouted over her shoulder. "Yee-hah! This is fun! I haven't done this in years, not since Toby and I were kids."

She clicked on the bike lights and wobbled out into the street, which luckily was completely empty, and careered down towards the town centre. Tam grabbed his old bike from the corner of the shed. Propped up against it was his toy sword, and without even thinking why he was doing it, he picked it up quickly and looped the belt round his waist. Then he jumped onto his old bike and pedalled after Aunt California. The bike was really small for him now; he had to pedal with his knees sticking out so they didn't bump against the handlebars.

"Keep up, Tam!" Aunt California shouted again.

"But where are we going?"

"I don't know yet! We're going to find Oban, wherever he is."

As it happened, they didn't have to look far. They were wobbling down the pedestrianized bit of the high street, weaving their way past all the strolling shoppers, when suddenly Tam shouted, "There!"

"Where?" Aunt California gripped the brakes and stopped the bike.

"Where all those people are!" Tam said.

He tumbled off his bike and ran over to an electrical goods shop. A small fascinated crowd had gathered outside it, laughing and pointing at something in the display window. Tam and Aunt California squirmed their way to the front. In the

window were several television sets, all different sizes. They all showed the same picture, a snow scene with huskies heaving sledges. Except for one, the biggest. Hunched up inside it, smiling and jabbering away as if he was telling the weather forecast, was Oban.

"I might have known," whispered Tam. "He loves television, Aunt California. He's always asking how the people get inside it. Even though he saw himself on the BBC News one day, he still couldn't understand how it happened. And now he's done it. He's magicked himself really small!"

"And climbed in through the back," Aunt California muttered. "He's a weird-looking guy, ain't he, with all that fluffy hair? Hey, wait a minute! How about if I go in the shop and *buy* that TV! He'll be trapped in there till we decide what to do with him. That'd be a nice bit of fun!" And she marched into the shop, leaving Tam to hold both the bikes.

It nearly worked. Tam watched from outside as Aunt California pointed to the window and the shop assistant climbed in past the other televisions on display there. He had no idea why everyone outside the shop was so interested in that particular set. He didn't look at the screen, just bent down and picked the set up. But a look of alarm spread across Oban's face. He fell over and looked around anxiously, sliding first to one side, then to the other. The watching crowd outside the window laughed, and more people gathered round to see what was going on. Some complained that the bikes were in the way, but Tam wasn't even thinking of moving yet. Now he could see that Oban was clutching something shiny behind his back. Just as the assistant swung the television out of the window space, a blue spiral swizzled round the screen, and Oban disappeared. Tam hopped up and down on tiptoe, trying to see what was happening. Now he could see the assistant blipping the remote control so the television flashed from channel to channel. There were husky dog scenes, reality shows, quiz games, old films, but no Oban.

Aunt California flicked her hand dismissively and shook her head. "No, I've decided I won't have it," she said, heading out of the shop. "Television's just a load of junk these days."

Tam saw the assistant bend down to pick something off the floor, then call Aunt California back. "Is this yours?" he asked. "Funny, it seemed to drop out of the television set!"

From where he was standing in the doorway, Tam couldn't make out what it was, but he saw Aunt California's face light up with smiles.

"Just what I was looking for!" she said, and tucked whatever it was inside her purple coat.

The crowd ambled away in various directions, full of laughter and wonder about the strange TV show they'd seen, and Tam and Aunt California were left to themselves. She swung back onto the bike as soon as they were in the street again.

"Climb aboard, Tam."

"Perhaps we'd better go back home for tea," Tam sighed. "It's getting pretty dark for fairy hunting."

"Jeepers creepers, this ain't no time for tea!" Aunt California said. "We won't lose him now. Didn't you tell me that he kind of lights up blue in the dark?"

"Yes, he does. Especially when he's angry."

"Oh, he'll be angry now all right." Aunt California drove the pedals down. "Let's move. You got that spider with you?" she asked over her shoulder.

"She always comes with me." Spinner ran down Tam's sleeve and tickled his hand.

"OK. Let me have her, just in case."

Mystified, Tam handed Spinner over to Aunt California.

"My, she's tickly!" his aunt said. "I'll keep her in my pocket, if she don't mind. Have you got that golden key you told me about?"

Tam patted his pocket. "Yep."

"Hand it over, honey."

"What are you going to do with it?"

"Isn't it obvious, Tam? Show me the way to the green passage. I'm going to get the old hag to call her son back home to Faery. I'm going to set her free."

The Green Passage

The green passage was the way to Faery.
It looked like a pile of heaped-up boulders
in a cleft in the hill, almost completely
overgrown with ivy and holly. Nobody
would know that there was a way through
there. But one day, nearly ninety years
ago, Great-grandpa Toby had seen the
king of the fairies coming out, and had
wanted to go through ever since. He
had sent Tam through with Pix to rescue
Blue last Midsummer's Eve. But there was
no way of getting between the boulders
now. Only fairy magic would do it. Great-
grandpa Toby had tried all his life, and the
only way through it was by magic. Tam
had been back there many times since,
and had gazed and gazed at the tangled

holly and scrambled over the boulders, but
he had never been able to find a crack
that was big enough to crawl through.

When they were near enough, Aunt
California switched off her bike light and
told Tam to do the same. She put her hand
inside her coat and drew out the little
silver and gold plastic windmill, and Tam
realized then that that was what Oban

had been holding behind his back when he was sitting inside the television set. She waved it round and round above her head.

"This," she said, "is the windspinner, Tam."

"The windmill?" Tam asked, puzzled. "But I always thought it was my bike that was the windspinner!"

"No. This is the special thing that your great-grandpa left for you. This is what your fairy friend wants more than anything in the world. Remember how much he loved the starburster? He could see magic things through it, because it made the world look different. Remember how he loved the humming machine? Just a bit of metal, but when he blew through it, he made his breath change into music! And now this little windspinner – swizz it round, and it makes the air move! Watch! Watch!" The more she swung the windmill, the brighter the air around it

became, like coloured strands of ribbon.
"It's making the wind spin, Tam! It's as
magic to King Oban as a fairy wand, and
he *wants* it, all for himself. He wants it so
badly! I'll show you."

She tucked the windspinner into its
holder on the handlebars and rode her
bike as fast as she could up and down the
path, making a dazzling whirr like
dragonfly wings in the winter darkness.

And in no time at all, a blue light
glimmered towards them through the trees.

"He's ours!" breathed Aunt California.
"We caught him, Tam."

The blue light turned back into Oban.
He was taller now. His skin was a shining
silvery blue and his eyes gleamed like
bright golden stones. He didn't look
anything like a mortal child now; he
looked terrifying. He stood in front of the
boulders with his hands on his hips. And
he roared with anger:

"Mine! Mine! Give me back my windspinner!"

Aunt California chuckled. "My, you've got a nasty little temper. Now just stand out of my way, dandelion-head. Me and Tam here are going through that passage."

"We can't," Tam whispered to her. "We have to have something velvet, something sharp and something silver!"

"We got 'em," Aunt California

whispered back. "Or we will have in a minute."

"But you have to be a nine-year-old boy to go to Faery. Great-grandpa Toby told me that."

"Hmm. We'll see about that. Why should boys have all the fun?"

"But it has to be on Midsummer's Day, or once in a blue moon," Tam went on.

"And how about New Year's Eve? Look at my watch, Tam. Close to midnight on New Year's Eve! Ain't this just about the most special day of all, when the old year creeps into the new and everything begins again? Past and present and future all rolled into one millisecond? If that ain't a good enough time for going to that Faery place, I don't know what is."

"But—"

"But nothin'!" She shushed him impatiently and advanced towards Oban.

"Now listen, whiz-kid," she told him. "This ain't no place for you. Your magic is all cock-eyed here. Where you come from, you're great and powerful, you have infinite magic and power, you can do anything you want."

Oban puffed himself up, glowing with pride.

"But here — pouf! You're nothing but a ball of blue fluff!"

Tam gasped. How could she talk like that to the magnificent King Oban?

Oban was listening, that was for sure. He seemed twice as tall, twice as grand, twice as terrifying now.

"Trouble is," Aunt California went on, "you've lost it. Your magic don't work no more. Ain't that so?"

"How dare you!" Oban said, his voice cold with anger. "Watch." He lifted one arm, and the grass under his feet burst into flames. Tongues of fire licked around him,

❉ 429 ❉

blazing into the night, as high as his waist, as high as his shoulders, higher than his head, and died away again. He stood where he had stood before, perfectly unharmed, inside a ring of scorched grass.

Tam had never seen anything so powerful and frightening, but Aunt California tutted with scorn. "That old trick! If I've seen it once, I've seen it a dozen times. You'll have to do better than that, Magic Mouse."

"Please stop," Tam whispered. "He might do something awful to us."

"No way," his aunt said. "I haven't enjoyed myself so much in years."

Oban raised both hands up to the sky. A shower of stars rained down all around them, brighter than jewels, quieter than snow, softer than feathers. It was the most beautiful thing Tam had ever seen.

"Hmm. Pretty nice," Aunt California conceded. "And it's worn you out, hasn't it?"

It was true. Oban had slumped to the ground, pale and exhausted. Aunt California marched right up to him and stood over him.

"What kind of a fairy is it who can't even put on a firework display without falling into a faint? I bet you haven't got one trick left, have you?"

"What more do you want?" Oban's voice was weak and quavering. It was obvious then that the king of the fairies was actually afraid of old Aunt California. He reached out his hand, trying to grasp the windspinner, but she snatched it away from him and laughed.

"Oh no you don't, bluebottle! If you are truly a fairy, I challenge you to perform one more trick." She twitched the windspinner this way and that, as if it was a tinselly wand and she was a pantomime fairy. "Turn me into a little girl again. Hmm? About nine years old. Can't do it, can you? Too hard for a stage magician like you."

Oban was dazzled by the windspinner. He held his hands over his eyes and struggled to his feet. Aunt California swizzled the windspinner backwards and forwards. "You are very tired," she said in a low, rich voice. "Soon you will fall into a deep trance. You will be hypnotized. You will do exactly as I tell you. You will perform the task that I have set you."

Oban couldn't take his eyes off the swinging windspinner. His stare became dazed, his eyelids drooped. He was breathing deeply, slowly.

"Now, Oban, mighty king of the fairies. Show us your greatest magic. Turn me into a little girl."

"Nothing is too hard for me," Oban answered. His voice, too, was slow and heavy, the voice of a sleep talker. He placed both hands on California's arms, and instantly she changed from an old lady into a little girl, with golden hair tied into plaits, short white socks and shiny silver shoes. Her huge purple fleece was a neat little velvet coat.

"Quick, Tam!" she shouted. "Climb on!"

She swung onto Tam's bike, and Tam scrambled onto his old one.

"Open! Open!" she shouted, driving the pedals down hard towards the green

swathes of holly and ivy. The windspinner whirred silver and gold on her handlebars, sharp as blades now. She steered the bike towards the green boulders. Tam raced after her, pedalling as fast as he could. He closed his eyes – surely the bikes were going to crash into the boulders – and then opened them again because he couldn't bear not to look. And silently, the boulders rolled apart. Aunt California cruised through into the green passage.

"Wait!" roared Oban, and for a second Tam paused and looked back over his shoulder.

"Stay with me!" Oban pleaded.

Tam turned again, and saw the boulders rolling together. With one last mighty push down on the pedals he squeezed through, just in time.

Behind him, Oban and the world of mortals disappeared from sight.

The Sleeping Soldiers

The guardian of the green passage stood
in front of them, barring their way with
his arms outstretched. His seaweed hair
floated around him like a cloak. The
sleeping soldiers were wide awake, clad in
armour, swords drawn. They had been
asleep for a thousand years, and they had
only risen from their slumbers to bid
farewell to King Tobit when he left Faery.
Now they waited anxiously to defend his
kingdom from the invasion of mortals.
There were hundreds of them. They filled
the long cave from side to side and from
end to end. They were dagger-eyed and
grim-faced, with thrusting, bristling beards.
They put their swords across each other to
form a barrier that nobody could cross.

"Jeepers creepers!" Aunt California breathed. "You never told me about these prickly porcupines!" She looked over her shoulder and winked at Tam. "Kind of fun, hmm?"

"Snix snee," the guardian snarled, showing his snaggly green teeth in a menacing grin.

"You know me," Tam said. "I'm Prince Tamlin! Remember! I have Vinand'r at my side!" He tried to draw his plastic sword from his belt, ready to hold it out so the guardian would change it from plastic to glistening steel. But nothing happened.

"I guess we need a little bit of good old-fashioned man-magic." Aunt California held the windspinner above her head. She whirled it around, trying to make its wings spin and whirr. It clicked a couple of times and then stood still. The soldiers advanced, sneering. "Do you know any better tricks, Tam?" she asked.

"Maybe there isn't enough air in the cave," Tam said. "We could try blowing very hard."

"Guess I might pass out if we do that," Aunt California said. "I always faint when I try to blow up balloons!"

Tam felt a sudden light movement on his wrist. Spinner had scrambled out of his pocket and was running across the floor of the cave towards the soldiers. She sprang up and deftly wrapped a thread round the legs of one of the soldiers, then another, and another, skittering frantically between them. She looped her silver thread behind her so, one after another, the soldier knights found that their legs were bound together.

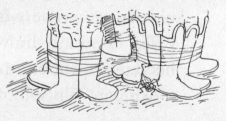

As soon as they realized what was happening, the knights started slashing their swords this way and that, striking themselves free of the web that was being cast around them. As fast as they struck, Spinner bobbed between them, lashing them together again.

"Careful, Spinner!" Tam shouted. "Don't let them chop your legs off!"

The cave was filled with the sound of whistling as the knights beat their swords against Spinner's thread. The air rippled as if a wind was gusting.

"Oh, you clever spider!" Aunt California pushed her bike nearer to the knights, holding the windspinner up high. In the whirlwind caused by the slashing swords, it began to spin, faster, then faster, showering the cave with flashing light. The knights stood still and gazed up at it, completely spellbound.

A great "Whee!" of amazement came

from them, and they lowered their swords. Spinner's threads snapped away from them, and they stepped aside to leave a clear passage. They lifted their swords to form an archway.

"Hail, Princess Califfa!"

"Do you mean me?" Aunt California laughed. "Princess Califfa! Why, I don't remember nine years old being such a load of fun!"

"Hail, Prince Tamlin!"

Aunt California led the way through the archway of swords, nodding from side to side and waving a hand as though she was Queen Elizabeth of England, and they passed right out of

the knights' cave and into the brilliant, glorious sapphire light of a fairy day.

"Jeeeeeepers!" Aunt California sighed. "My, oh my, this is so swell! I really am . . . I really and truly am in the land of the fairies." She glanced over her shoulder. "Come on, little spider. I'll give you a lift."

She scooped up the exhausted Spinner, who hummed cheerfully and snuggled herself into her sleeve.

"No tickling! OK, we're off!" Aunt California stuck the windspinner into its holder on the handlebars, and drove her feet down on the pedals. "Now, which way, Tam? Where do I find that old Damson-hag?"

Tam looked around, trying to remember how he had reached the Damson-hag's grotto. Pix and the little elf, Morva, had taken him on a frightening journey through the forest of soldier trees, he remembered, and they had led him to meet the Flame-reader. And *he* had set a series of tasks that had to be completed before Tam could find the Damson-hag. What were they? Something to do with a silver path? Something to do with a feather?

"I can't remember," he said at last. "I wish Morva and Pix were here. They'd know."

"*Wish, wish, a fairy wish,*" sang Spinner, and instantly the air seemed to tremble around them and a green elf ran and tumbled round the wheels of the bikes. "Plince Tamlin back! Plinpless Califfa come!" he shouted.

"I guess you're Morva!" Aunt California said. "How did you know we were coming?"

"Waiting all days long," Morva said, somersaulting with

pleasure. "Waiting Plince Tamlin and Plinpless Califfa come."

Wings fluttered around them, and a voice called, "This way! This way! Follow me, but hurry, hurry, hurry." A fairy with purple eyes swooped alongside them.

"Elva!" Tam laughed. "Aunt California, this is the fairy who threw my starburster in the pool! But she's my friend now."

"My, you're beautiful, just like Tam told me," Aunt California said. "I've heard so much about you." She turned her head from side to side as Elva fluttered all around her. "But can't you stop still a minute? I'm getting dizzy, just watching you."

"No time to lose," Elva said urgently. She

flew in front of them,
waving her arms to urge
them on.

"I'm going as
fast as I can."
Aunt California
pedalled her short legs up and down. The
windspinner whirred like insect wings on
the handlebars. "Is this the way to the
Damson-hag's grotto?"

"No time yet for the Damson-hag.
You've come to save us. I knew you would
come. But hurry."

"But what do you mean, we've come
to save you?" Tam asked, panting along
behind Aunt California. "What from?"

"From the Flame-reader," Elva said.
"You must ask him to spare us."

Tam stopped pedalling. "The Flame-
reader. I never want to see him again,
Aunt California. I told you how
frightening he is."

Aunt California stopped too. "No, we ain't here to see no twiggy monster like him. We're here to free the Damson-hag and tell her she's got to get your king back, so we can take my brother home. That's what we've come for, and that's what we'll do. OK? Take us to the old hag's grotto, and then we'll leave you to sort yourselves out. I ain't getting mixed up with no Flame-reader, no sir."

Morva wailed in despair. He jumped up and clung onto Aunt California's handlebars.

"You must help us," Elva begged, twisting backwards and forwards around Aunt California's head.

"Stop buzzing around and tell us what's going on," Aunt California said.

Elva held out her wings and hovered in front of the two bikes. "The Flame-reader is so angry with us for letting King Oban go away that he's turning us all to ice."

"Jeepers," sighed Aunt California. "That ain't nice, is it, Tam?"

"Already the people of the palace have been frozen," Elva went on. "The queen and her servants are all ice-statues in the garden, with frozen vines and brambles growing over them. There is no way for us to turn them back again. We don't have enough magic. It's our turn next, that's what he told us. Everyone. Maybe even you, now you've come here."

A voice seemed to rise up out of the earth and the air, booming and echoing around them.

> *"Ice, ice, my kingdom will freeze,*
> *all will be ice to its very heart.*
> *All creatures in it,*
> *all birds of the air,*
> *all fishes in the streams,*
> *all flowers and trees,*
> *ice, ice, all will be ice, for ever."*

Morva and Elva shuddered, clinging to each other.

Aunt California turned to Tam. "I guess we have to find a way of helping these guys," she said.

"I know," he said. "But how can we do it?"

"Speak to the Flame-reader. Please, please, speak to him. Please ask him to spare us," Elva begged. "He will destroy Faery. Princess Califfa, Prince Tamlin, please, please hurry."

The Enchanted Forest

Aunt California twiddled the windspinner for a bit, thinking hard. Then at last she said, "OK. We'll speak to the boss first. And then we'll free the hag. Which way do we have to go?"

"Emble Fost," Morva whispered.

"That way," said Elva. She pointed ahead to a forest of huge green trees.

"Fine. Lead on."

But Morva gibbered and shivered with fright, and Elva covered her face.

"They daren't," Tam said. "They're too frightened to go on, Aunt California. And so am I. I just don't want to go in there."

"Hmm . . ." Aunt California stared at the gloomy forest. "Ain't too scary, Tam.

Just a bunch of old trees. What's in there, anyway?"

"The forest has grown up around the fairy palace," Elva told them. "You have to go through it to get there. And that's where the Flame-reader is, somewhere in the forest, if you dare approach him. He's a burning tree, so he will never freeze."

"I dare approach him all right," said Aunt California.

"But he might turn us to ice!" Tam said.

"Trust me, Tam. I'll think of something. Come on, let's get to the palace and find out what's going on there."

"But don't stop," Elva warned her. "Don't stop for anything, whatever you may see."

"I want to talk to my brother first, before I do anything else."

Aunt California didn't notice the anxious look that Morva exchanged with Elva.

"Poor Kingie Toble," Morva sighed, and Elva put a finger to her lips.

"The sooner we get this over with, the better." Aunt California spat on both her palms and rubbed them together. "Here we go!" she shouted. "Come on, Tam! Let's show that bunch of twigs what we're made of! *Hoi!*"

And she set off with a fierce battle cry, waving the windspinner over her head. Tam felt his bike being pushed from behind by Morva and pulled from in front by Elva. At last they let go, and he found himself hurtling along behind his great-great-aunt.

"Good job I've got nine-year-old legs instead of eighty-nine-year-old ones," Aunt California puffed. The windspinner sizzled as they cycled. Soon they swung into the emerald forest, into the deep dark gloom that was as black and cold as the bottom of the ocean. Strange, still shapes loomed in the branches; bright eyes stared like coloured glass. Tam paused for a moment and reached up to touch one of the shapes, and realized they were birds, turned to ice. The forest was completely

silent. The trunks of the trees, the branches, the twigs, the leaves were as motionless as the stones in a graveyard.

"Everything's made of ice," he whispered. "Everything!"

Aunt California bent down and touched the ground. Blades of grass snapped in her fingers, and the sound echoed like a pistol shot in the silent forest. "Yeah," she breathed. "Spooky, Tam. But we can't stop now. Come on."

On and on they pedalled, and at last they could see the white marble towers of the palace. And there they stopped.

"Now, Tam," said Aunt California. "I'm going right on in. You don't have to come if you don't want to. You can wait out here." She gazed at the flight of marble steps that led up to the palace. "But I'm going in."

"Then I'm coming with you," said Tam.

"That's my boy."

Aunt California and Tam left their bikes at the bottom of the marble steps and climbed bravely up to the door. They walked into the great hall and gazed around. There was no singing now, no laughter or children's voices. A deep silence, like a held breath, hung over the palace. Frozen spider webs dangled over everything like white veils.

"My, this is eerie, this place," Aunt California whispered.

She tiptoed through the queen's chamber and Tam followed; *tap-tap* went their feet, echoing like tiny drums in the silent hall. They went out into the garden. Nothing moved there, no sound, not a breath. All the beautiful beds of flowers were spiked with white ice. Stiff weeds and brambles tumbled over boulders in the grass.

So many boulders, thought Tam. I don't remember seeing so many before. With a start, he realized that they weren't boulders at all. They were statues. He ran from one to the other, breaking away the frozen weeds, lifting up brambles to peer at the white, icy faces.

"I know them," he sobbed. "I know them all. They've all been turned into statues."

Several small figures were humped together, some holding hands and standing

on the tips of their toes as if they were skipping. They were children, fairy children, turned to ice as they were dancing. The tall figure with sweeping icicle hair was Queen Tania. The little one with her wings stretched out as if she was trying to lift herself up and fly away was Pix. Tam turned to Aunt California, the tears streaming down his face, but she wasn't looking at him. She was kneeling down in front of the ice-statue of a boy.

"This is Toby," she sighed. "My dear brother Toby, I've come all this way to find you, and you're turned to ice! Can't

you see me?
Can't you
hear me at
all?"

She gazed
into the ice-
statue's blank
eyes. Was she
imagining it,
or did they gleam for a moment, as if they
knew her?

There was a sudden whooshing sound,
and the whole sky lit up with orange, red,
gold and yellow streaks, as if it had been
set on fire.

"*Ice, ice, my kingdom is ice!*"

"It's the Flame-reader," Tam whispered.

"OK." Aunt California stood up. "Then
we'd better go and speak to him."

She turned back just once to look at
her frozen brother, and followed Tam out
of the palace garden.

The Burning Tree

Tam and Aunt California hadn't walked far before they saw a burning tree blazing in the heart of the green forest. It seemed impossible that a tree could burn when everything around it was frozen, but Tam knew that it was caused by great magic. He walked resolutely towards it. As he drew near, he felt the heat from it scorching his face and eyes like a bonfire. The light was blinding, but he stared right into the heart of it. There he saw the face of the Flame-reader.

"I am Prince Tamlin," he said. "Why are you turning everything into ice?"

There was no answer, except for a whoosh of flame. He stepped back. He could feel Spinner tickling his neck.

"Ask no questions," she whispered.

Tam tried again. "Great Flame-reader, please melt the ice. Please turn everything back again."

The Flame-reader laughed, sending huffs of smoke out of his mouth. "You ask me to break the spell, and yet you have stolen my son?" he roared.

"Your son?" Tam turned to look at Aunt California, then back again to the Flame-reader. "I don't know what you mean."

"You took my son with you into the land of mortals, and you left a mortal in his place," the Flame-reader roared. "You have destroyed Faery."

"Your son? Now I know! You are Oban's father!" Tam said.

"I am the father of the king of the fairies."

"So what do you think you're doing, turning yourself into a firework and all

your people into ice-cubes?" Aunt California demanded.

"Ask no questions," Tam reminded her.

"Piffle!" she shouted. "Just listen to me, hot-head. Your son left this place of his own accord, and do you know why?

Oh, you don't answer questions. Well, I'll tell you why he left. Because you wouldn't let him do what he wants to do! He's the king, not you, and yet you stop him playing with all these toys that he loves. Yes, toys. That kaleidoscope, that harmonica, this little plastic windmill here – there's nothing magic about them. You know that very well, don't you? They're toys, and he wanted to play with them. You've spoiled his fun, and no wonder he ran away. He's the king here, not you. What do you mean, *Ice, ice, my kingdom is ice*? It ain't your kingdom in the first place! You've got to let him rule his kingdom the way he wants to. Let him bring his friends here if he wants. That's what I think. It's not Tam who's destroying Faery. It's not Toby, or Oban, or anyone else. It's you, you great sparkler. And it's time you were put out!"

Tam looked at Aunt California in amazement. How could she dare to speak to the Flame-reader like that? And how could she say that the starburster, the humming machine and the windspinner were just toys, when they had made so many magical things happen? He felt like crying. Any minute now the Flame-reader would cast his spell on them, and they would be blocks of ice for ever. Why wouldn't she shut up? With every new thing she said, the Flame-reader huffed and humphed, blazing with rage, gathering his magic together.

Aunt California backed off, waving his smoke away from her face. "Jeepers, I've always hated smokers!" She turned round and winked at Tam. "Time for a little real magic!" she whispered. "What do you say, Spinner?"

Spinner bobbed along the handlebar and jumped off, anchoring her thread so that it stretched and swayed behind her, and then she swung round and round on the end of it, a little silver blob making swift circles in the air.

"*Spin, spin, a mighty wind!*" she sang. "*Twist and spin! Spin and twist! Fan the flames, higher, higher, magic the wind, put out the fire!*"

"Get it?" Aunt California asked Tam. "Can we do it, d'you think? Can we go fast enough?"

"Course we can!" said Tam, suddenly understanding everything. Aunt California was making the Flame-reader angry on purpose. And now it was a battle of his magic against their magic; his fire against their wind. They had to magic a wind that was greater than his fire. "We can do it! Can I take the windspinner, Aunt California?"

"Sure! It's yours, Tam." She tugged it off her own handlebars and stuck it onto Tam's. "Good luck! Away we go! One, two, *threeeeee!*"

They cycled rapidly round and round the Flame-reader's tree. Never in his life had Tam pedalled so fast. His legs ached, and still he drove the pedals down. Round and round the flaming tree they cycled.

"Spin, spin, a mighty wind!" he yelled.

The windspinner gathered speed till it was just a blur of light. Tam tugged it off his handlebars and held it out towards the tree. He was so exhausted, he could feel his bike tilting; he could feel himself falling towards the flames.

"Keep going! Keep going!" Aunt California panted behind him.

Tam summoned up all his strength. His legs were like pistons, pumping up and down.

"Fan the flames, higher, higher, magic the wind, put out the fire!" he shouted.

And at last it happened. There was a great soaring *whooosh!* And the flaming tree was enveloped in a black tornado. It spiralled round the tree, forcing the flames higher and higher. The tree was trapped inside the tornado. The Flame-reader's face disappeared; his voice stopped.

Sparks showered away from the top of the tornado, and wherever they fell, the ice began to melt. Trees moved their branches, flowers opened up, birds began to sing again. Further away, the fairy statues stretched their arms, fluttered their wings, opened their eyes. Tam dropped his bike and ran back to the garden to watch. Pix was one of the first to thaw. She squealed with excitement.

The queen's icicle hair began to drip like a mermaid's. She raised her hand and lifted it away from her face. She opened her eyes and gazed around dreamily. "Where's my king?" she murmured. "Where's Oban?"

"Perhaps her memory's still frozen," Tam said. "She's forgotten all about King Tobit."

"He's not moving!" Aunt California wailed.

It was true. Toby was still an ice-boy, frozen solid, staring ahead of him. The sparks hadn't reached him.

Tam cycled back to the flaming tree. The tornado had almost died down now. It was just a few spiralling wisps, nothing like the spinning fury of a few moments ago.

"More!" Tam shouted desperately. "Just a few sparks more! Please!" He whirled the windspinner round, sending acrid smoke into his mouth and his eyes. He could hardly see, but he kept on waving it madly round and round, and at last the tornado gave a little weak spurt, and a shower of sparks bloomed out like a fountain. Tam caught them in the blades of the windspinner and ran to the far end of the garden, where his frozen great-grandpa was crouching. He held the windspinner over the ice-statue's head and whirled it once more. The sparks fell out;

the ice around Great-grandpa cracked like a hatching egg, and fell in broken pieces to the ground. Toby stood up slowly and then kicked his legs high in the air.

"My word, I can move again!" He did a quick somersault. "Ah! That feels better!"

"Want to go home?" a voice asked.

Toby turned round and stared at the little girl on Tam's new bicycle. He peered at her, scratching his head. "You're not who I think you are, are you?"

"Why, who do you think I am?" asked Aunt California.

"My bossy little sister!"

"Sure am!" She beamed.

And they hugged each other just a little, because nine-year-old boys and nine-year-old sisters don't really like hugging each other much. They grinned as if their faces were going to crack, because they were so pleased to see each other.

"How did you get here?" Toby asked.

"Oh, a bit of this and a bit of that and a lot of magic windspinning."

"Your windspinner's brilliant, Great-grandpa!" Tam said. "I mean, King Tobit!"

"My word, I've had enough of that. I'm ready to go home, if we can get there," Great-grandpa Toby said.

"You know you won't be nine years old any more, when you go home? Or you, Aunt California?" Tam reminded them.

They nodded. "That's fine by us," Aunt California sighed. "We'll be dignified, for a change."

"My word!" chuckled Great-grandpa Toby. "I'm not making any big promises like that!"

"Well, anyway, we ain't going home yet," Aunt California said. "We came here to do something very important, didn't we, Tam, and we've still got to do it. We have to free the Damson-hag so she can call Oban home to Faery. Spinner, you run in front. I guess you'll be able to find her. After all, it was you who wrapped her up. Follow me, boys. If you dare."

The Damson-hag Is Free

Spinner scuttled in front of California, showing her the way to go, darting through trees that were dripping with thawing ice. "*Hurry, hurry,*" she sang.

Ahead of them streaked a red fox. "Follow the stinking fox!" Tam shouted. "I remember him – he led the way for me last time."

The fox turned his head and looked at Tam, and there was a flash of recognition in his eyes. Then he plunged on into the dense green forest. And suddenly he stopped, sniffing the air eagerly.

"Can you hear

something creaking?" Aunt California asked. "Wait a minute."

Now they could all hear it, and as they hurried nearer, they could all see it. A golden cage was hanging from the branches of a tree, and a figure bound up in silver thread was hunched up inside it.

"The Damson-hag," Aunt California said. "We've found her. She looks pretty harmless, all trussed up like a chicken."

And as they approached the cage, the hag looked up and saw them. Her eyes seemed to burn right into Tam with such hatred that he was scared to go any further.

"What will she do to me, Spinner?" he whispered. "She locked Great-grandpa in a cage and wanted to keep him there for ever. She tried to lock me in a cage. She could do anything to us if we let her go."

But however frightened he was, he knew he had to set the Damson-hag free.

It was the only way to bring Oban home, to give the land of Faery its true king again. Tam didn't belong anywhere else but in Faery. He thought of Morva and Elva and Tanta and all the fairies and elves – his friends. He thought about little Pix, dancing about excitedly in the palace garden. They needed to be safe again, with their real king.

Aunt California and Great-grandpa Toby came and stood behind him.

"Are you sure you want to let her go?" Great-grandpa said. "She's a nasty piece of work, my word she is. She enchanted me and locked me in that cage for long enough."

"We have to let her go," Aunt California said. "She's Oban's mother. She's the only one who can help him get back to Faery. Go ahead, Tam."

Tam took a deep breath. "Go on, Spinner," he said. "Undo your magic web."

The little spider darted up to the cage. She worked as quickly as she had ever worked, undoing every stitch she had made. Untwisting, unravelling, unbinding, unthreading. And all the time she worked, the Damson-hag never took her raging purple eyes off Tam. At last every thread had dropped away.

Aunt California stepped forward and took the golden key out of her pocket.

"Do it," Tam urged her.

Trembling, she fitted the key into the lock of the cage, and turned it.

"I release you, mother-queen of the fairies," she said. "And I beg you to call your son home again."

The door swung open, and the Damson-hag uncurled and stepped out. As she did so, her age fell away from her, just as Spinner's threads had done. She was her young self, with deep dark purple eyes and long hair the colour of damsons, which fell around her shoulders and down to her feet in gleaming strands. She moved like a dancer, slim and supple and lithe.

"Jeepers creepers," California said. "You're really, really beautiful."

The Damson-hag smiled at California. There was no more anger in her eyes, no more hatred, no revenge. "Thank you for freeing me. You are welcome here, little girl," she said. "You have made me whole again. You have broken the Flame-reader's spell of ugliness and age, of evil and cruelty. I will be young for ever now, as fairies should be." She turned to Great-grandpa Toby and kissed him. "I'm sorry I locked you in the cage. The music you played on your magic humming machine was so beautiful that I wanted to be able to

hear it all the time. When you played, you made me young, you made me dance. For a moment or two I was a fairy girl again. I wanted to keep you here for ever, to make me young again. But you don't belong here. I should never have tried to keep you. I will never be evil again."

"Hmm," said Aunt California. "I don't know whether to believe you or not. I guess this place will be pretty boring if there are no baddies around."

For half a second, a snarl swept across the Damson-hag's face, then disappeared as quickly as a cloud skipping across the sun. She smiled at Aunt California. "Depends how much meddling goes on," she said. "I am, after all, the mother of all fairies."

"That's what we wanted to ask you," said Tam. "Please, please, can you use your magic to bring Oban back home? We can't do it, and he can't do it. And the fairies need a king, and he wants to come home."

"And I want to go home too," said Great-grandpa Toby.

"Easy, easy, easy!" The beautiful mother of all the fairies opened her arms wide and called, "Oban! Oban! Come home."

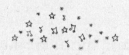

Home

Oban was sitting on a rock, staring at the boulders that blocked the way to the green passage. Then he noticed a light bobbing through the darkness. He turned his head. Someone carrying a torch was coming towards him. He could hear a voice calling.

"Are you there, lad? Come home!" It was Tam's dad's voice. "Come home, Tam! Come home!"

And he heard another voice, echoing from far, far away.

"Come home, Oban! Come home!"

Round and round the voices echoed.

"Here! Here!" Oban called. "I'm here." He held out his arms, and felt himself being lifted up, rushed through the air, moon high, star high. He laughed out loud. His old magic had come back! He was going home.

As if he had been there all the time, Oban blossomed out of the air in front of the Damson-hag.

"Oh boy!" Aunt California whispered. "That's real magic, that is! And he doesn't look like an overgrown school kid with a spiky mop on his head. He looks – like a king!"

She was right. Oban was tall and magnificent in his white shimmering cloak. He bowed to his mother and kissed her hand, then turned his golden eyes on Aunt California. She curtseyed nervously.

"These are the children who set me free," the Damson-hag said. "Be kind to them, Oban."

"Of course," King Oban said. "They are welcome in my kingdom."

He put both his hands on Tam's shoulders. "This boy taught me how to play," he said. "And this boy" – he turned to Great-grandpa Toby – "this boy helped me to make my dream come true."

Toby scratched his head. "Well, you made my dream come true, your majesty. Tobit, king of the fairies! My word!" he chuckled. "But if you don't mind, I'd like to go home now."

They all walked together to the

palace, the Damson-hag with her arm tucked into Oban's, Aunt California and Great-grandpa Toby giggling together, and Tam and Spinner.

"Will you come with me, Spinner?" Tam asked. "Or will I have to leave you here?"

Spinner jiggled up his leg and hid in his pocket. They were suddenly surrounded by the fairies and elves, cheering and dancing because their true king was home again.

"Hail, King Oban!" they called. Pix tumbled around him in excitement, half flying, half skipping, and the queen stretched out her arms and ran to her husband. "My king! You've come home to me!"

"I'll never leave you again," Oban promised. "I am King Oban, king of the fairies. I will never meddle with man-magic again." He shuddered. "And

I never, ever want to go to the land of mortals again."

He turned to Tam. "But Tam was a very good friend to me. We had fun, Tam, didn't we?"

Tam nodded. He didn't like to mention how difficult Oban had been. But he was right. It had been fun, especially at school, till Christmas and the windspinner. That was when things had started to go wrong.

"Can you still spell?" he asked.

"Of course he can cast spells," said the Damson-hag. "He's the king of the fairies."

But Oban knew what Tam meant. "Abcdefghijklmnopqrstuvwxyz. K–i–n–g O–b–a–n."

Aunt California cheered and clapped her hands, and King Oban bowed proudly.

"But I never learned how to ride a bike," he said sadly. "Some things are just too hard, even for me."

"Jeepers, the bikes!" Aunt California said. "We'd better go fetch them, Toby. Can't leave them behind!" She ran off, calling over her shoulder, "Betcha can't pedal as fast as me!"

"Bet I can!" Toby shouted, running after her.

"Califfa has been a wonderful friend to us," Queen Tania told King Oban. "She and Tamlin saved us from the Flame-reader's spell. We were turned into ice-statues. If they hadn't been so brave, the whole kingdom would have been turned to ice. Tamlin and Califfa broke the spell. They burned away the Flame-reader's wicked magic, and we'll never be cursed by him again."

She pointed to the Flame-reader's tree. The fire had burned itself out completely now; the fury of the tornado had died away. Yet the tree stood untouched. Not a leaf was scorched, not a twig had been burned. Leaning against its trunk was a very old man. His hair and beard were as white as snow, and stretched right to the ground. His eyes were as grey as wood-smoke, his skin was wrinkled and brown. He held out his bony hand to Tam.

"Farewell, Prince Tamlin!" he called. His voice was so weak that Tam could hardly hear it.

"Who are you?" he asked.

"Don't you know me?" The old man laughed sadly. "I'm the oldest fairy of them all."

"The Flame-reader?"

"Oh, I can't do that now. Can't read flames, or make spells, not now. Gone, gone, all my magic. Gone, my spells and my power. Just a tree-man now, looking after the king's forests."

Tam realized that he had asked the old Flame-reader two questions without being roared at. He decided to risk a third. "Can I ask you another question?"

"Oh, ask away, ask away. I like to have a question to answer."

"Long ago, you gave me your little spider, Spinner," Tam said nervously. "I just wondered, if it's all right with you, if she could come home with me?"

The old man stretched out his hand, and Tam fished Spinner out of his pocket and put her into the wrinkled palm.

"Little Spinner," the Flame-reader mumbled, his old face creasing into smiles. "Tam, you should know that it's not possible. Don't you remember what you were told, the first time you came here, when you first crossed the sapphire lake? *Nothing take from Faery. Nor food nor drink take, nor sleep have. Go wisely, go bravely, young prince.* Do you remember that?"

Tam nodded. His throat was starting to ache; his eyes were blurring with tears. He knew exactly what the old man was going to say.

"You have been very wise, and very brave, young prince. And what have you learned since that time?"

"I've learned that fairy things belong

to Faery, and mortal things belong to mortals. Man-magic and fairy magic don't mix," said Tam.

"And what did you tell Oban about our magic, when he went with you to your land?"

"I told him that fairy magic is dream magic."

"And so it is, Tam. Spinner will be in your dreams."

The old man limped away, with his spider bobbing from his wrist. Tam rubbed his eyes and turned away, to see Aunt California come screeching up on his bicycle, ringing the bell loudly. Great-grandpa Toby ran behind her, pushing Tam's old bike, with Pix sitting giggling on the saddle.

"California says it's time to go, Tam," Great-grandpa said. "But it looks like you'll have to ride your old bike, I'm afraid . . ."

"I liked him when he was King Tobit,"
Pix whispered to Tam. "Can't he stay?"

"He can't stay here. He doesn't belong
here," Tam explained. "And I've got to
go too." He lifted Pix off his bike and
climbed on.

"Don't go. Don't!" Pix clung to the
handlebars.

"I want to go home," said Tam. "I want to see Mum and Dad and Baby Blue."

"Will you come back?"

Tam shook his head. "No. Never. I don't belong here." He gazed around him, taking in all the beautiful colours of the flowers that were blooming again in the garden. In the Faery twilight they glowed like jewels. He turned back to Pix. "I'll never see you again, Pix. I have to stay in the mortal land now. Soon I'll be ten, and I won't be able to come back here."

Pix sobbed loudly. "But you're my best, best friend. You looked after me when the fairies left me behind in your house. You brought me here. You turned me back from an ice-statue."

"But you have your own magic, Pix," Tam said. "You turned Great-grandpa Toby into a nine-year-old boy. You flew me here, all on your own."

"But that's because I was with you!" Pix sobbed. "I can't do any magic without you!"

"But you will. You have to stand on your own feet." Tam pushed her gently off his handlebars. She tumbled backwards, then fluttered her wings and landed neatly.

"See!" Tam clapped. "You can do it!"

King Oban came over to them and drew Tam to one side. "Brave young Tam," he said. "I will make a promise to you, but no one else must know of it. I will give you a special, secret power. Sometimes, not often, when you look through your starburster, on nights when the stars are as blue as sapphires, you will see Pix, and she will see you. Sometimes, very rarely, when you play your humming machine, she will hear your music and dance to it. And sometimes, for an instant, when you make your windspinner turn, you will hear her voice singing. You must never share this knowledge with anyone else, or you will lose it."

"Thank you," said Tam. He knew how hard it would be not to share such a secret with Great-grandpa Toby, or Aunt California, or Mum, or Dad, or his friends at school. Aunt California rang her bell again. Toby climbed up behind her, tucking his arms round her waist.

"Farewell!" The voices of Queen Tania, King Oban, Pix, the oldest fairy of them all, the mother of all fairies, Morva, Elva and tiny, singing Spinner, all rose around them like a cloud of chiming light.

"Bye!" Aunt California called.

"Bye!" Great-grandpa Toby shouted.

Tam paused for a moment when he reached the entrance to the green passage. He made sure the windspinner was tucked firmly in place on his handlebars, then turned for one last look behind him. "Goodbye, land of the fairies!" he said softly. Then he drove his pedals down towards the dark green gloom of the cave.

A Strange Tale to Tell

"Tam! There you are! What are you doing out here in the dark, eh? I've been looking everywhere for you. Didn't you see my torch, lad? Didn't you hear me calling you? You shouldn't be out on your bike at this time of night!"

The light of the torch dazzled his eyes. Tam put on his brakes and drew up close to Dad. He felt as if he would burst with grinning, he was so pleased to see him.

"Is Blue all right?" he asked.

"Blue? Course she is! She's been in bed a long time since. But your mum will probably have fetched her down by now for her last feed," Dad said. "And you'll never guess what's just happened. When I was walking down the path here looking

for you, I was nearly knocked down by a
bike. Seemed to come from straight
between those big rocks there! And guess
who was riding it? I thought it was two
kids at first, and I was just about to shout
at them. But no, it wasn't kids at all! It
was your great-great-aunt California and
your great-grandpa Toby! He's come
home, Tam. After all this time, he's
come home to us!"

And when Tam and Dad got back to the house, there was Great-great-aunt California on one side of the fire.

"Jeepers creepers," she said. "This is good. I'm just warming my weary old bones."

On the other side of the fire was Great-grandpa Toby. Baby Blue was on his knee, stroking Great-grandpa's prickly chin and gurgling sleepily.

"There you are, Tam! Just in time for toasted teacakes," said Mum. "Get yourselves nice and cosy, you two. Great-grandpa Toby is going to tell us where he's been all this time."

Great-grandpa Toby took a bite of teacake and wiped the butter off his whiskers with the back of his hand. He looked across at Tam and winked.

"My word, we'll be up all night!" he said. "I'll be telling you such a long, long story. And your mum and dad won't believe a word of it. Will they, Tam?"

And, of course, they didn't.